Metaphorosis

January 2020

edited by
B. Morris Allen

ISSN: 2573-136X (online)
ISBN: 978-1-64076-161-2 (e-book)
ISBN: 978-1-64076-162-9 (paperback)

Metaphorosis
a magazine of speculative fiction

from
Metaphorosis Publishing

Neskowin

Metaphorosis

January 2020

Beautifully made speculative fiction

Also from Metaphorosis

Score – an SFF symphony

Reading 5X5: Readers' Edition
Reading 5X5: Writers' Edition

Best Vegan Science Fiction & Fantasy

Best Vegan SFF 2018
Best Vegan SFF 2017
Best Vegan SFF 2016

Metaphorosis Magazine

Metaphorosis: Best of 2018
Metaphorosis: Best of 2017
Metaphorosis: Best of 2016

Metaphorosis 2018: The Complete Stories
Metaphorosis 2017: The Complete Stories
Metaphorosis 2016: Nearly Complete Stories

Monthly issues

by B. Morris Allen

Susurrus
Allenthology: Volume I
Tocsin: and other stories
Start with Stones: collected stories
Metaphorosis: a collection of stories

From the Editor

This issue marks our first step into something new – occasional serials! L. Chan's novella *Sonata* kicks things off, with part I at the end of this volume, and parts II and III coming in February and March respectively. Each serialized portion is a self-contained unit, but you'll have the most fun by reading all three parts. We did!

January 2020

Kozuna, the Ogre's Child

Felicity Drake

The red rental car plunged into the tunnel. Hitomi's eyes adjusted: the sun winked out, replaced by the yellow glow of sodium lights flashing by too fast.

Professor Ueda had insisted on driving. Hitomi had offered, of course, but he had looked so indignant that she was reluctant to offer twice. For an elderly man, he was a remarkably reckless driver. The tunnel was narrow and winding, and if she'd been driving, she would have taken the curves much slower. But then, living in Tokyo, he probably didn't have many opportunities to speed down an empty road. He must have been enjoying himself.

"Are you excited for your first fieldwork, Sasaki?" Professor Ueda asked, raising his voice to be heard above the roar of the engine echoing in the tunnel.

"You'll stay with me, right? When I'm interviewing her?" she asked.

"You'll mostly be listening, not interviewing," Professor Ueda reminded her. "But of course I'll supervise."

When Hitomi had first started her master's in folklore, she had thought that no one went into the countryside trying to collect folktales anymore. Professor Ueda had assured her that there were still a few remote corners where old stories, beliefs, and practices lingered, if you knew where to look. Now that she was starting the fieldwork for her thesis, she imagined herself joining the pantheon of folklore pioneers from previous centuries, like the Grimm brothers or Yanagita Kunio, tromping out into the countryside to capture the last traces of oral tradition before they disappeared forever.

As they emerged from the tunnel, her eyes hurt from the sudden brightness of the sun. The village spread out around them. Its neat emerald gardens were strung with silver and gold streamers to keep away the crows; its distinctive steep thatched roofs were familiar from the black and white photographs she'd seen in old reference books. Utterly unchanged. How incredible that a place like this could exist, just a day's travel from Tokyo.

It was August, which should have been high tourist season for this sort of mountain getaway, but the streets were mostly empty. Hitomi saw a single bent-double grandmother working in a garden, with a single family of tourists snapping photos of her.

"Looks like they could use some help with marketing," Hitomi remarked.

"Fewer tourists are better for us," Professor Ueda assured her. "Easier to get a sense of the village itself. Once the tour buses arrive at a village, it's usually impossible to do any real fieldwork."

They cruised through the heart of the village, passing the Mountain Heritage Museum, the Farming Tradition Center, and half a dozen restaurants and guesthouses. As they drove, the houses grew farther apart, and the trees encroached on the village from all sides. The road narrowed, then turned to gravel.

At the end of the road, there was one last house before the mountain rose up again, steep and thickly wooded. A thatched-roof farmhouse, like the others in the village. But the wood was darker and damper, the eaves sagging, the thatch visibly balding.

"Is this it?" Hitomi asked. There was no sign, nothing indicating that it was a guesthouse.

"There's always some hardship in fieldwork, Sasaki," Professor Ueda said, with some relish. The car crunched over the gravel and came to a stop. Before he got out, he squinted at the rearview mirror, whipped a comb out of his pocket, and combed his sparse hair into neat rows.

A gray cat was sleeping on the stones that led up to the front door. As Hitomi picked her way carefully towards the house, the cat woke and stalked towards her, lifting its head as if demanding to be petted.

"Hello, beautiful," she cooed, crouching down to oblige it. The cat nuzzled her hands, then flopped down on the stone and sprawled out, displaying its fuzzy white stomach.

Ahead, the front door rattled as it slid open. The cat mewed, padding back over to the door and winding itself around the ankles of the man who appeared there. His jeans were rolled up to his knees, showing his bare, furry legs.

Hitomi's first impression was of sheer size. The man was so tall he had to duck slightly to fit through the door, and he had big ungainly hands like boulders. Once she'd gone to a museum in Ryōgoku, where the sumo stadium was, and seen what had to be a sumo wrestler on his off hours, shuffling shyly into a convenience store as if he were embarrassed of his hugeness. This man reminded her of that, massive but standing with his shoulders modestly hunched.

The man bent and picked up the cat, letting it climb onto his shoulders. Hitomi's eyes followed the cat up to his face. He looked only a few years older than she was, somewhere in his thirties. It was difficult to tell, because his ruddy face was obscured with thick black stubble.

"You're the guests? Ueda and Sasaki, two rooms, three nights?" he demanded.

Hitomi's soul withered and died at the thought of anyone calling Professor Ueda plain *Ueda*, as if he weren't a tenured and published and profusely awarded scholar, the sort of man who got to make the first comment at all the monthly meetings of the Tokyo Folklore Study Group.

"That's right. And you are?" Professor Ueda answered, taking out his handkerchief and wiping his glasses on it, apparently unruffled.

"Kiyama Tatsuya. I'll carry your bags," the man announced. Without asking, he went back to their rental car, opened the trunk, and hoisted their suitcases. Hitomi was an overpacker in general, indecisive about which clothes and shoes she'd want on a trip, plus she had packed several of the books she was reading for her thesis. Her suitcase was so heavy that one of the conductors had had to help her lift it onto the luggage rack in the train. But Mr. Kiyama hefted it in one hand as if it were weightless, and carried Professor Ueda's two bags under the other arm, all without disturbing the cat riding on his shoulders.

Professor Ueda raised his eyebrows at her, as if to say, 'Welcome to fieldwork!'

Hitomi followed the man to one of the guestrooms, where he deposited her suitcase on the tatami mats, carefully, like a giant setting down a tree trunk.

"Thank you, Mr. Kiyama," she attempted.

"Just Tatsuya. Dinner's at six," he announced, and turned to go. She wasn't sure if meals were supposed to be included, and she was especially not sure if she wanted to spend an entire meal sitting across the table from this odd stranger. There was something off-putting about him, something she couldn't quite put her finger on. But before she could figure out what to say, he was already closing the door.

The mats had the sweet, grassy smell of real tatami, but they were faded and a little musty, probably not replaced as recently as they should have been. The futon was already spread out on the floor, neatly made with flowered sheets and a padded quilt that looked handsewn. There was a little alcove with a tiny glass vase full of fresh flowers. It was hard to imagine a man like Tatsuya making beds and picking wildflowers, but she supposed that was part of running a guesthouse.

Although her door was closed, she could hear the muffled clatter of pots and pans, and she could smell something faintly savory. She went out into the front room to investigate.

The storyteller was there.

Sitting comfortably on a cushion was a tiny old woman, so small that her body seemed to disappear inside her kimono, until all you could see was the soft round peach that was her head, topped with sparse white fuzz. She sat beside a traditional hearth built into the floor, with an iron kettle hanging on a chain from the ceiling.

There was a more modern kitchen off to the side. From the well-loved patina of the appliances, Hitomi guessed it probably dated back to the sixties or seventies. In this narrow kitchen, not much larger than the one in her parents' apartment back home in Tokyo, Tatsuya was standing at the stove, stirring a pot. His massive, hairy arms were especially incongruous against the daffodil-yellow apron he was wearing as he cooked.

She realized she was staring—although to be fair, he was difficult not to stare at.

"Dinner," he explained tersely. As if that was what needed explanation.

It was a little funny to see someone so enormous and so decisively male fussing in a kitchen. Her ex-husband had never cooked.

Tatsuya, his brow knit in concentration, set aside some of the vegetables and ran them through a blender. She guessed that he was preparing mushy food for his grandmother, who might not have enough teeth left to chew fibrous vegetables.

Hitomi realized all of a sudden how much she was inside someone else's home, how intimate the whole scene was. She froze at first, trying to think of what to say, but Professor Ueda breezed past her into the front room and sat across from the old woman as if it were all quite natural.

"Mrs. Kiyama," Professor Ueda began.

"Everyone calls her Grandmother," Tatsuya interjected from the kitchen.

Grandmother inclined her head in apparent agreement.

"Grandmother," Professor Ueda said. "My name is Ueda, and this is my graduate student Sasaki. We've heard that you know a lot of stories. Would you be willing to tell us a few?"

"After dinner," the old woman declared. "I never tell stories before sunset."

Or at least that's what Hitomi thought she said. Grandmother's dialect was so thick, she could hardly be sure.

"A sensible practice," Professor Ueda nodded.

Although Hitomi had worried that the dinner would be too awkward to bear, sitting across from Tatsuya (a silent, sullen mountain), the food itself was remarkable. Plain mountain fare: a bowl of rice, homemade pickles, cold tofu, stewed vegetables, and buckwheat soba noodles. But everything was fresh and subtle and perfect. She'd never had soba with such intense flavor or such lovely, springy texture; she suspected that someone in the village must have made it by hand.

And once Grandmother had her dinner, she was an endless fountain of chat. Her accent was so heavy that it was hard for Hitomi to follow, but she got the general idea. Grandmother attempted to introduce the village to her two citified visitors, explaining that the village one ridge over had been made a UNESCO World Heritage site, and *they* got heaps of tourists in the summer, but the houses in the Kiyamas' village weren't as well-preserved, so they had been passed over. Which was apparently a source of some grief to the local restaurants and guesthouses. She'd run this house as a guesthouse for forty years, doing all the cooking herself, but these days it was all up to her grandson, and they didn't get many customers, since they hadn't been able to rethatch the roof as often as it needed, and the neighbors' guesthouses were in better condition. But, she added, these two guests were clearly discerning travelers, because she was the only one left in the village who knew the old stories.

"No one else in the world knows these anymore," she boasted sweetly. "They don't have these stories in the next village. And no one else here remembers them all —I'm the last one left born in the Meiji period."

"You were born in *Meiji*?" Hitomi gasped, forgetting her manners for a moment in her surprise.

"June 1912," Grandmother nodded. "Just one month before the Emperor Meiji died."

Hitomi had never met anyone born in the Meiji period before. There couldn't have been many left in the whole country. She noticed that Grandmother, whose eyes were still sharp, seemed rather gratified by her awe.

"My, it's getting dark already," Grandmother observed, with an air of great ceremony. Shadows were gathering at the corners of the front room, and the cooler night air was seeping in through the old house's walls.

"I'll make tea." Tatsuya knelt next to the old earthen hearth, arranged wood in a neat pile, and started a fire. He filled and rehung the iron kettle above the fire.

He turned off the electric lights in the kitchen when he filled the kettle, so that the only source of light in the house was the flickering flame of the little fire starting in the hearth. The kettle swayed slightly on its chain, making shadows waver on the dark wooden walls.

Hitomi felt the hair on the back of her neck stand on end. This was not at all like sitting under fluorescent lights in the library, reading an edited collection of folktales with helpful annotations. It was a performance, an important one, one Grandmother had been repeating for decade after decade.

"Excuse me, Grandmother," Hitomi put in. It felt almost sacrilegious to interrupt with reality. "May we record your stories?" She held up her phone.

"Go ahead, if you like. Now, what sort of stories do you want to hear, children?" Grandmother began, settling herself comfortably on her cushion and accepting a cup of tea from Tatsuya, who then receded into the shadows behind her, like a black-clad stagehand.

Professor Ueda, at sixty-eight, was indeed young enough to be her son. He only smiled. "Why don't you tell us your favorites, Grandmother?"

Grandmother launched into a long series of practiced, well-loved stories. Hitomi recognized some as cousins of tales she'd read in collections, but others were wholly new. Kappa, ghosts, forest fires, disappearances, babies delivered by the gods, good little girls and bad little girls, mountain deities and mountain demons.

As Grandmother continued telling her stories, Hitomi lost track of time. It surprised her when Grandmother hid a yawn in her sleeve and reflected: "Well—I think there's time for one more story tonight." Her eyes narrowed in a smile. "Do you want to hear the story of why our family is called Kiyama?"

Hitomi found herself leaning forward, entranced by the sparkle in the old woman's eyes.

Just then, the electric lights popped back on with an audible buzz.

"It's past nine, Gran," Tatsuya announced, a little too loudly. "You're usually in bed by now."

"Oh, I suppose," she sighed. "More stories tomorrow night, then."

Grandmother allowed Tatsuya to lift her from her cushion and help her into her bedroom.

In the electric light, the front room looked shabby, the fire pitiful, and all the veils of mystery had departed.

"Wow," Hitomi whispered to Professor Ueda, who answered with a boyish smile.

"There's nothing else like it, is there, Sasaki?"

That night, Hitomi curled up underneath the padded quilt with her phone. It was so silent and dark in the house. She was used to the streetlights and traffic noise of her neighborhood in Tokyo. The light from her phone, at least, was a thread connecting her to the real world.

She texted her parents to let them know that she had arrived safely and to wish them a good night. Then she settled in to browse the internet; she was too keyed up to sleep.

Do you want to hear the story of why our family is called Kiyama?

She had known that the guesthouse was called Kiyama Guesthouse, but she hadn't seen how it was written. Now that she thought about it, she wasn't sure what characters the name Kiyama was made of; 'yama' was obviously mountain, but 'ki' could be any number of things. It wasn't a common name. She searched for the guesthouse online, and after a while found its listing on a travel site:

Minshuku Kiyama, spelled 鬼山. The 'ki' was an alternate reading for the word 'oni,' or ogre.

Ogre mountain.

When she was a child, she had mostly thought of oni as cute cartoon figures: bright red skin, huge eyes, wild hair, that silly tigerskin loincloth they were always wearing in children's books. It wasn't until she'd started her degree in folklore that she saw the grotesque images of them in older illustrations. The way people had once imagined ogres, back when people took such things seriously.

She thought of a picture scroll she'd read just last semester, a sixteenth-century story about an ogre in the mountains outside of Kyoto. He would go down into the city at night to abduct young maidens and bring them to his mountain dwelling, where they became both the servants and the main dishes at his luxurious, depraved banquets with his ogre friends. She had been shocked by the graphic violence in this prettily painted little scroll. Cups full of sparkling human blood. Ogres chewing on girls' naked thighs. A platter full of girl sashimi.

Ogre mountain. There was definitely a story behind that name.

In the center of the formica table in the kitchen were two full plates and a scrawled handwritten note:

GRAN IS SLEEPING.

KEEP IT DOWN. SOUND CARRIES.

Tatsuya's hospitality was somewhat lacking. On the other hand, when Hitomi peeled back the plastic wrap covering her plate, she discovered a fluffy omelet, a salad with neatly halved cherry tomatoes glistening like rubies, and a little knot of a roll studded with raisins. It was a breakfast any housewife would have been proud of.

"What are our plans for today?" she whispered to Professor Ueda. She didn't want to wake Grandmother.

"I suspect Grandmother won't tell any more stories until sunset," he mused, neatly buttering his roll. "You have some time to yourself until then. Why don't you go out and explore the village?"

"Isn't there fieldwork I ought to be doing?"

"That *is* fieldwork. Walk around the village, talk to people, write down your observations. Even if you never use this material in your thesis, it'll help you write. Folklore only exists in context."

"And you?"

"I promised the curator at the Mountain Heritage Museum I'd pay him a visit. I'll meet you back at the house before dinner."

Hitomi slipped an apple into her backpack (she didn't feel bad about it, because there was another messy handwritten note beneath it reading "YOU CAN TAKE THESE") and headed out the front door.

The village felt different on foot and by the morning light. Flowers smiled at her from everyone's garden. Inspired by Professor Ueda's exhortation, she took photos of all the flowers she didn't recognize, and resolved to look them up in a botanical manual once she got back to the library. It might be important. Anything might be important!

She had never had time to think about flowers before. The last year of her marriage, she had tried to make a date with her ex to see the cherry blossoms in Ueno Park, and he had kept pushing the day back, saying he was too busy to take the time off work. By the time they both had a Saturday free, the blossoms had already fallen.

Closer to the center of town, one of the local stores was open. There was a woman out front, setting out a sign advertising different varieties of homemade tofu. Unable to make up her mind, Hitomi ordered three different kinds: hiya yakko, cold and topped with soy sauce, scallions, and bonito flakes; dengaku, grilled and glazed with miso; and ganmodoki, a fried tofu-vegetable fritter. The woman delivered her tofu and sat across from her to keep her company as she ate, and they got to chatting.

"Have you lived here long?" Hitomi asked, which turned out to be a stupid question, because the woman just wiped her hands on her apron and chuckled. Everyone in the village had been born there; no one had moved there. Although plenty had moved away.

"Where are you staying?" the woman asked.

"At Minshuku Kiyama," Hitomi answered, pointing back up the road to where it disappeared in the darkness. Somewhere in those shadows was the old house.

"Oh." The woman's mouth worked slightly, as if she were trying to restrain herself from informing this outsider that Minshuku Kiyama was the worst guesthouse in the village.

"I came to hear Mrs. Kiyama's stories," she explained.

"*Ohh*," the woman nodded in understanding. "They're a unique pair, those two."

"Mrs. Kiyama and her grandson?"

The woman nodded again. "He's a good boy, really. He puts the snow tires on our car for free every year, won't think of taking money for it. But there's funny blood in that family, always has been, that's all."

Hitomi ate her three kinds of tofu and listened to the woman's stories about the village, which weren't at all like Grandmother's; they were about whose guesthouse went out of business, or who the mayor used to be before the village was disincorporated, or whose children had moved away to Tokyo and didn't visit as often as they ought to. Hitomi nodded and urged her on when she could. Before she left, she bought vacuum-sealed packs of smoked tofu to give to her parents and classmates as souvenirs. Then she strolled back up the road to the Kiyama house, hurriedly taking notes on what she remembered of their conversation, although she doubted that the tofu-seller's gossip would make it into her thesis.

Beside the house, Tatsuya was stretched out underneath some enormous piece of farm machinery.

"You okay under there?" Hitomi asked, peering down at his feet sticking out from under the machine.

"Fine. Just fixing." He rolled out from underneath the machine and sat up. His face was smeared with grease, and his hands and forearms were black up to the elbow.

Part of fieldwork is getting to know the people, she reminded herself. *Folklore exists in context.* And Tatsuya was part of that context. He had grown up hearing Grandmother's stories, breathing the air in that house. He and the stories were inseparable.

"What's that called?" she asked.

"Combine. For harvesting rice." He frowned and rested his elbows on his knees. "Hand me that cloth?"

She found the rag he was gesturing to and handed it to him. He tried to wipe the grime off his hands.

"Is it yours?" she asked. She hadn't seen rice fields around the Kiyama house.

"Neighbor's," he answered, fiddling with the rag. "This is my work."

"Oh—you're a mechanic?"

He nodded. "Only one in three villages. Only one young enough to do it, I guess." He paused, staring not at her, but at a spot in the distance somewhere off to the left of her head. As if he were frightened of looking directly at her, she realized. "So you're a researcher?" he ventured.

"Sort of—I'm not really anything so impressive. I'm just a student."

He blinked and didn't say anything, so she kept going.

"I mean, I'm in graduate school. I'm a little old for it. I started my master's at twenty-nine. Everyone else in the seminar is younger than I am, which is a little awkward. All the girls act like I'm their big sister, even though I've been out of school for so long that actually I'm always asking them for help..."

"Why folklore?"

"Sometimes I think I looked at the course catalogue and chose the most impractical, most useless degree," she joked. Mostly joked. "I used to work in finance. It was really, really practical. Totally real-world. Real money, real problems, real deadlines. And so for a few years I worked twelve-hour days doing real, important stuff, and I broke out in hives all over my body, and then I quit."

Her stomach clenched in embarrassment, and she realized she had just vomited up her life story to him. At least she had managed to leave out the divorce. He didn't seem particularly fazed by any of it, just nodded thoughtfully.

"So you listen to stories instead?"

"Yeah," she agreed, and she couldn't quite hide her smile. Breathing fresh mountain air, eating the world's best tofu, and listening to people's stories: it was ridiculous, but that was her job now. Placing things in context. A great big jumbled puzzle that was this village and its past, with Tatsuya as one funny jagged piece of it. "Actually, I was wondering if you could help me sometime. I'm going to need to transcribe the recordings of your grandmother's stories, but I have some trouble understanding her accent..."

"I bet." Tatsuya had a strong regional twang, but he was comprehensible. His grandmother had probably been raised in a time when even the schoolteachers still spoke dialect, and she might not have had much schooling at that.

"Would you help me transcribe? I don't know how I'm going to find someone back in Tokyo who could do it."

"Sure, no problem." He nodded solemnly.

A bell rang faintly from inside the house. Tatsuya glanced over his shoulder, then set down his greasy rag and closed his toolbox.

"Gran's up. Guess she needs help."

"You take good care of her," Hitomi observed.

He glanced back at her; for a moment, he looked as if he were about to say something. Then he just awkwardly grunted his assent. "Dinner'll be ready at six," he added, and disappeared inside.

People probably didn't notice him often, she thought. How often would he meet new people at all, here in the village? Here everyone had known him since birth, had a whole narrative to explain him, and would never have an occasion to experience the pleasure she just had, seeing for the first time that there was something sweet in him. That he might be kind.

Context.

"Tonight, you'll do the talking," Professor Ueda informed Hitomi.

"Are you sure?"

"You're ready. It'll go well. And I'll be there if you need help."

Hitomi glowed with pride. If he was letting her take the lead on the fieldwork, it meant he trusted her judgment. He was going to use these recordings for his own publications, too, after all.

"My, my—it's good to have the house full of young people," Grandmother sighed, as Tatsuya helped her shuffle to her customary cushion.

Hitomi started her phone recording and folded her hands in her lap.

"Grandmother, will you tell us more stories tonight?"

"I'd be happy to. Tatsuya, will you pour some sake for our guests?"

Like the night before, Tatsuya started a fire, filled everyone's cups, turned off the electric lights, and receded into the darkness behind Grandmother. The fire cast a web of shadows over the wrinkles and divots in her face.

"What kind of story do you want to hear?"

"Tell me a story about the village, please," Hitomi urged.

Although she had already told them stories for hours the night before, Grandmother resumed her performance with undiminished energy. Her voice rose and fell. She was a child, a barking dog, an exiled samurai. For as long as Grandmother spoke, her stories were the only reality. Hitomi forgot about her thesis research, forgot about Tokyo. Time slipped away.

"I think there's time for one more story tonight," Grandmother finally murmured. "What would you like to hear?"

Last night, Grandmother had tried to tell a story about the family name. Kiyama, Ogre Mountain. There had to be a great story there—but was it all right to ask for it? Something so personal? She saw Tatsuya leaning forward in the shadows, his hands on his knees as if he were getting ready to spring up.

If she didn't know this story, if she left the village without hearing it, she would regret it forever. There wouldn't be a second chance. Grandmother was 103, and no one else knew her stories...

The fire spat sparks at the iron kettle. Grandmother waited for her answer.

"Can you tell me the story about the Kiyama family, Grandmother?" Hitomi asked.

The old woman's face creased into a smile. "That's a good one. I'm glad you asked."

Behind her, Tatsuya stood, but before he could reach the light switch, Grandmother raised her little pink hand in a wordless command. Tatsuya sank quietly back to his knees on the mats and didn't move again.

Grandmother closed her eyes and began, her voice low and deliberate:

Long ago, hundreds of years ago, in this very village, in this very family, there was a mother and a father with just one daughter. She was a great beauty, and they wanted only the best for her. But this was a poor family then—is still a poor family now—and their beautiful daughter had to help her parents earn money. She used to go up to the mountain to gather brushwood to sell in the village. It was a sad sight, to see this lovely girl climbing down from the mountain with her back bent from carrying brushwood, but all the village said it was wonderful to see a daughter so devoted to her parents.

But one day, the daughter didn't come back down from the mountain. The whole village searched for her day and night for a week, but they couldn't find her. The parents were beside themselves with grief. Although the rest of the villagers accepted that she was gone, her father did not, and every day he went into the mountains looking for her. The house fell into disrepair as he neglected his work to search for his missing daughter.

After months and months of searching, one day he slipped through a crevice in the rocks and found himself inside an ogre's cave. Inside the cave, he found his daughter—pregnant.

"Quick," the father said. "Come with me. I'll take you home."

But the daughter said, "No, it's not safe. My husband the ogre will come back to his cave any second. You've got to hide."

So she hid her father inside a chest in the cave, and not a moment too soon, because just then the ogre returned to the cave.

"It stinks like human in here," the ogre growled.

"Of course it does, darling; I'm here," the daughter answered.

"I smell *two* humans," the ogre insisted.

"Then you must be smelling the child in my stomach," the clever daughter suggested. "He's human too."

The ogre accepted this answer, and he sat down to eat his dinner of human flesh. The father waited, terrified, inside the chest, all night long. And in the morning, after the ogre left the cave, the father and the daughter escaped back to the village together.

The daughter never dared to climb the mountain again, and lived safely in the village for the rest of her days. But a few months after she returned from the ogre's cave, she bore his child. A child who grew to be like all the Kiyama men, a great big strapping boy like my Tatsuya there. And all the village knows there is still ogre blood in the Kiyama family, and that is how we got our name.

Grandmother picked up her cup and drained it of sake, breaking the spell of her story with a satisfied sigh.

"Then do you believe you are descended from an ogre, Grandmother?" Hitomi asked.

"Oh, no. I married into the Kiyama family," she answered brightly. "My Tatsuya is the last one in the village with ogre blood in his veins."

Across the room, in the dim firelight, Tatsuya's dark face was flushed red. Red like an ogre's face, his coarse hair wild, casting shadows on the wall almost like a pair of horns—

"That reminds me of a famous story from the northeast," Professor Ueda began. After a drink or two, he was often inclined to start lecturing. "Grandmother, have you ever heard of a story called 'Kozuna, the Ogre's Child'?"

"Tell me," she urged, her eyes brightening. "I don't hear new stories often these days."

It was well past nine, but she didn't look at all tired. Tatsuya made no attempt to hurry her off to bed. It was probably too late for that; the damage had already been done.

"The story of Kozuna, the ogre's child, begins very much like your story. An ogre kidnaps a girl and makes her his wife. Her father goes looking for her, and finds her on Ogre Island."

"Ogre Island?" Grandmother protested. "Everyone knows ogres live in the mountains."

"You have a good point," Professor Ueda conceded politely, "but there are quite a few stories from other regions which are very clear about Ogre Island. At any rate, the story continues as your story does, with the daughter hiding her father from the ogre. Then they escape, in this version by boat. But the ending is different.

"I heard this ending in a town in Iwate Prefecture. The ogre's child is named Kozuna, and as he grows older, he realizes that he has an ogre's hunger for human flesh. Finally, unable to control his hunger, he chooses to take his own life rather than devour his neighbors. He asks the villagers to burn his body so that nothing remains. But after they burn him, the ashes of his body drift into the wind, and even his ashes still hunger for human flesh. And that is the story of where mosquitoes come from."

"Oh—that poor boy," Grandmother murmured, shaking her head in sorrow, as if the character in the folktale were real.

Tatsuya was sitting behind Grandmother, still and massive as a statue. His craggy face had the plain, decent ugliness of a carved wooden mask. Hitomi felt suddenly that she had been wrong to ask for the story of the family's name.

"If you've finished your drink, Gran, let's get you to bed," he rumbled.

"More stories tomorrow night," she assured them cheerfully. Perhaps she didn't have an audience as often as she would like. It was a long trek into the mountains to visit her, after all, and she had a century's worth of stories she needed to get out.

"I look forward to it," Professor Ueda enthused, bowing his head deeply. "Goodnight, Grandmother."

Hitomi stopped her phone recording. She quashed a momentary impulse to delete that night's file. She wanted to tell Professor Ueda that she wished they hadn't come, that she wished he hadn't let her lead the fieldwork.

"You did well, Sasaki," he declared, standing and heading to his guestroom.

"Thank you, Professor." She waited for his door to close before she stood. She turned the electric lights back on in the kitchen and washed up the sake cups and a few lingering dinner dishes. Tatsuya didn't reappear, even after it had been more than enough time for him to put his grandmother to bed. He might not have wanted to talk, after that.

Hitomi slipped out the front door. He wasn't there, but she heard or sensed something out in the darkness, and tried to feel her way around to the side of the house.

"You're going to break your neck walking in the dark like that. You don't know your way here."

A spot of light shone from the darkness to her left. She saw Tatsuya sitting on a rock by the edge of the woods, holding up his phone to light the way for her. Why hadn't she thought of that? She pulled out her own phone and illuminated the ground in front of her, picking her way carefully over to him.

Once she reached him, he made room for her on the rock next to him, and she sat. Neither of them spoke for a while. She resolved that she wouldn't speak first. It would be easy to babble something stupid, maybe even make things worse while she was trying to make things better.

Silence stretched between them.

"What's it like in the city?" he asked, finally.

"Have you ever been to Tokyo?"

"Never. I lived in Nanto for a while." Nanto was the nearest city to the village, actually a conglomeration of seven villages that had merged after their populations dropped. It wasn't much of a city. It was hard to imagine that anyone could live in Japan without seeing Tokyo, but she supposed it would be a long, inconvenient trip from this deep in the mountains. And he had his grandmother to care for.

"Did you like it?"

"Hated it," he answered quickly. She stayed silent, waiting to see if he'd continue. "There's no high school in the village. I went to the high school in Nanto, and it was so far I had to live in a dormitory."

"Must have been hard being so far from home at that age."

"I'm not good with people. I don't like to leave the village." He wouldn't look at her, just stared at his enormous hands in his lap.

"Don't you get lonely here?" she asked. "If there really aren't any other young people?"

"There used to be other people my age. They all left. Nothing here for them."

"But you...?"

"If I leave, there's no one to take care of Gran. Or fix things. Or help out the old-timers."

"But how are you going to find a Mrs. Kiyama?" she asked. Stupid, again. Her preparation for fieldwork hadn't taught her how to stop asking stupid questions.

"Last year, Gran learned that there are agencies that can send you a wife from the Philippines over the internet. Now every time she sees me on the computer she badgers me about ordering a pretty wife."

"Are you considering it?"

He shot her a dour look out of the corner of his eyes. Apparently not.

It was several minutes before he spoke again, and then all he said was: "I won't pass it on." Without a goodbye, he stood and stalked back off into the house.

It was so dark in the mountains, a pressing kind of darkness unimaginable in Tokyo. Hitomi clutched her phone, stared at the circle of light it cast at her feet.

Kozuna, the ogre's child, was terrified that he couldn't control himself, that one day he would find himself eating human flesh and he wouldn't be able to stop... She shivered. It was as if Tatsuya really believed it.

I don't like to leave the village, he'd said. *I'm not good with people.* As if what he meant was: *I don't trust myself around them. It's not safe for me out there. They're not safe around me.*

That night, Hitomi had three texts from her mother, but she didn't text back, not even to tell her about the magnificent tofu she'd eaten.

Back in the Meiji period, a prominent philosopher, Inoue Enryō, had attempted to convince the backwards nineteenth century populace that the supernatural wasn't real, that ghosts and kappa and ogres were just stories. It had always amazed Hitomi that this had been a real scholarly endeavor, that fairy tales had once been so deeply rooted that anyone had to do what Inoue Enryō did.

But here was a twenty-first century man who believed absolutely in the existence of ogres. No—who believed that he himself was an ogre. It was outrageous, and still...

Hitomi noticed with some distress that there was no lock on the inside of her guestroom door.

She felt a tickling on the back of her neck and reached back to rub it. When she pulled her palm back, there was a smear of blood on it. She had to swallow a scream—it had just been a mosquito. She'd crushed it with her hand, without meaning to.

She was losing it. Ever since they had left that tunnel, nothing had been normal. She had to get back to Tokyo, where the laws of physics still operated, where the night wasn't as black.

In the morning, there were fresh pancakes waiting on the breakfast table for her and Professor Ueda. No sign of Tatsuya or Grandmother.

"What did you think of that story, Professor Ueda?" Hitomi asked.

"Which one?"

"The origin of the family name. Do you think it's true?"

He chuckled warmly. "The mountain air is working its magic on you, Sasaki."

"I don't mean the part about the ogre— but is there any historical truth to it, do you think?"

Professor Ueda swirled his spoon in his coffee cup thoughtfully. "In villages like this, many of the local legends and stories are tied to historical fact. I know of some cases where local folklore has been corroborated through temple records. But all this story implies is—well, a single mother. A woman, a disappearance, a baby with no father. I suspect that sort of thing was just as common in premodern times as it is today."

It sounded so sane when Professor Ueda described it. He had probably encountered similar stories before; he'd done fieldwork in places much more remote than this. It was only her inexperience that was spooking her.

The night before, she'd dreamed that she was in the woods, and there was something invisible in the dark taking great big juicy bites out of her...

"I'd like to take the car today," Professor Ueda added, cutting a neat wedge out of a pancake. "There's a museum in Nanto I'd like to visit. You're welcome to come along if you want, but it's unrelated to your thesis project, so I'd encourage you to stay in the village."

"I'll keep exploring," Hitomi agreed. She wondered if he was leaving her alone in the village on purpose. In all his stories about the adventures of his younger days, he had been out on the mountains and islands by himself. Perhaps that was an important part of fieldwork: encountering the unknown by yourself without backup.

She stood outside the house and waved goodbye to Professor Ueda as he drove away. He was susceptible to a certain amount of fawning from his students, and it was only polite, after all.

Once the car disappeared, she stood on the stepping stone outside the front door and pondered. She had the day to do what she pleased. Grandmother wouldn't tell any more stories until sunset. She could have gone out into the village again, tried to find another villager to chat with.

But that seemed silly after what had happened last night. There was only one piece of context that really mattered after that.

Tatsuya was half underneath the combine, scowling at it while he worked.

Hitomi found a metal bucket and turned it over to make a stool, taking out her phone and her notebook. "Care to help me transcribe? Will that interfere with your work?"

"Go ahead."

They spent the morning working their way through Grandmother's recordings. Hitomi was careful not to play the one about the Kiyama family name. He translated from dialect to standard Japanese for her, explaining the local words for moss or mushroom. As long as she didn't say the word 'ogre,' he seemed happy enough to help.

"This must be different than working in finance," Tatsuya observed. "Are you happy, now that you left your old job? Is this what you like to do?"

"Honestly, on my worst days, I feel like the world's biggest loser."

He grunted disapprovingly.

"But it's true! Just last year, I had everything someone in my position could expect to have. A good job. A husband with a good job. A nice apartment. And I just set it all on fire."

"You were married?"

She nodded. "Three years. It seemed like a good idea at the time. We got along so well back in college, back when we were just dating. But once we got married and moved in together, it got... well, it was like I stopped being Hitomi and started just being a wife, to him. He wouldn't wash a dish or fold a shirt. Forget cooking or ironing. And I was working just as many hours as he was! It was just—you know, I never wanted to be a divorcée. But the divorce was the best decision I ever made."

She didn't know why she was telling him this. But he nodded seriously as he listened.

"So anyway, by any objective measure, I'm a loser. I'm thirty, already divorced, unemployed, living with my parents, spending a fortune on a degree I can't use for anything. But—" She shook her head. "But on the good days, I feel like—I don't know, like an adventurer. Like Momotarō." That was an unfortunate choice of folktale; Momotarō was famous for slaying ogres. "Like I just got into my little rowboat and paddled out into the open sea. And I left behind everything that was safe and stable on dry land, and I don't know where I'm going... but I'm totally free. And I'm kind of proud of myself for being so brave. Does that make sense?"

"It's not easy to leave things behind," he murmured. "I think the second version of your life story is better."

Tatsuya took a break from his repairs to cook lunch. He delivered a tray of soup and rice porridge to his grandmother, then returned to the kitchen.

"I could keep working on the combine, but there's no hurry." He hung his yellow apron on a hook. "It's hot today. It'll be cooler in the woods. We could go pick mushrooms."

"You know how to pick wild mushrooms?"

"Sure. Gran taught me."

In the entryway, Tatsuya paused by the door and pulled out a pair of clumsily handmade bracelets, colorful string and little bells.

"To warn off bears," he explained, and handed her one to wear. He was careful to drop it into her outstretched palm, as if he were avoiding any chance of accidental touch.

He led her up past the house and the garden, up the mountain's slope through the trees. It wasn't long before any trace of the village disappeared behind them. Hitomi realized she had become hopelessly lost within just minutes; she wouldn't have had an easy time finding the house again.

"There's no path," she pointed out.

"Not enough people come up here to wear a path. It's fine. I know the way."

"You come up here a lot? By yourself?"

"Free food all over the forest if you know how to look. Plus, it's quiet."

Sunlight filtered through the leaves overhead, then dimmed as the trees closed in around them. The forest was thick, and it was difficult for Hitomi to walk through the undergrowth. She regretted not changing into jeans and sneakers. Tatsuya, despite his size, slipped through gaps in the trees as if they were made for him, while she was stumbling and getting her skirt stuck on prickers. He noticed her trouble and started making sure he cleared a path for her, holding branches out of her way and warning her of logs or rocks underfoot.

"I've never been anywhere like this," she admitted. "I've been in the woods before, but... not like this. This isn't like Yoyogi Park. It feels like—like the woods aren't used to having humans in them. As if when I passed through that tunnel, I entered another world entirely."

"Like an alternate universe."

"Yeah."

"I like sci fi," he offered. "Old stuff. I like anything with outer space."

"I wouldn't have guessed that." There were little things about him that were oddly charming: his affection for the cat, his housewifely yellow apron, his handmade bear bracelets, his sci fi fandom. If he hadn't had an ogre's face, an ogre's body, an ogre's name, he would have been almost sweet.

They walked for what must have been an hour. She didn't want to check the time on her phone, didn't want to allow reality to intrude.

Although Tatsuya was carrying a basket, he didn't often stop to inspect mushrooms. Mostly he just walked in silence. His silence, or his clumsy, abrupt attempts at conversation seemed less awkward in the woods. It let her hear the birdsong. Occasionally he pointed to trees or birds or flowers and named them for her. She'd never heard the names before, but she wasn't sure if that was because of her general ignorance, or if he was speaking in dialect.

He stopped at the base of a broad tree and pointed to a cluster of squat mushrooms. "These are edible. Do you see how the ridges here..." He paused and looked up. There were little tapping noises all around them: raindrops on leaves.

"I guess I should have checked the forecast," Hitomi said.

"Sky looked clear when we started," he frowned. "Better head back."

Abandoning the unpicked mushrooms, Tatsuya headed back down through the trees. Even without a path, he seemed to know exactly where he was going. He was so much faster moving through the thick forest that he often had to stand and wait for her.

"How much longer until we reach the village?" she asked. A fat raindrop plopped onto the tip of her nose.

"It's an hour's walk at a good pace. There'll be mud; you'll have to take it slower going downhill." He scowled up at the sky. Even through the leaves, she could make out the dark shapes of gathering clouds. "Better hurry."

Hitomi followed him downhill. The rain was starting in earnest, and it was a struggle to keep pace without losing her balance on the wet leaves, the newly slick ground. She kept having to wipe the water out of her eyes, and then she took one wrong step—she lost her balance and came down hard on her left knee.

Tatsuya turned back, as if to help her up, then recoiled. Hitomi was suddenly aware that blood was welling up out of her scraped knee. She tried to wipe it clean, but only succeeded in smearing dirt and blood all down her shin.

"Rain's only going to get worse," he announced, staring off into the distance.

As if he were afraid even to look. "We'd better wait it out."

Hitomi couldn't imagine where they could shelter from the rain; there were no paths, no shelters, and the rain cut through even the thick trees. But his eyes were sharper, more accustomed to the woods, and he pointed to a rock formation not far away.

They were close to the naked mountainside, she realized, where the rocks formed a natural overhang that would keep off some of the rain. The rain pattered down harder, and by the time they made it to the overhang, it was pouring. Hitomi pressed herself back against the cool rock and shivered. Her skirt was soaked through, clinging wetly to her thighs, her scraped knee.

"Good idea," she whispered to him. "I wouldn't have liked walking for an hour in this."

It rained and rained. Tatsuya sat at the base of the rocks, his eyes closed. He looked utterly natural there, like a boulder that had just come loose from the mountain.

Hitomi poked around the cliffside, making sure to stay under the overhang. Water was pouring down like a curtain from the edge of the cliff, so she only had a narrow strip of dryish earth to explore. She took photos of the dripping wildflowers, the sodden moss, and the slick rocks. The flash of her camera shone off the cliff in an unexpected way.

"Hey, look at this." She tossed a pebble at Tatsuya to make him open his eyes. "I think there's a cave here."

"What?"

"Look. There's an opening in the rocks." It wasn't easy to spot, but there was a break in the mountainside, a spot that curved inwards. She tried to aim her phone inside, but it only illuminated a few feet.

She expected him to warn her about wild animals living in the cave, or something like that. Certainly he knew more about the forest and what was safe and dangerous than she did. But he didn't say anything at all, just walked up to the entrance of the cave and squinted at the inky blackness inside.

"It would be drier in there," she pointed out.

He didn't seem to hear her. He drifted inside the cave without looking back.

She followed, turning on her phone's flashlight. She swung the beam around the cave as she entered. It went back farther than she'd expected. It was surprisingly spacious inside, and pleasantly dry. Musty and dark, yes, but not smelly or dirty like she'd imagined an animal's den would be.

Tatsuya kept walking, moving forward blindly without a light until he stumbled on something.

"Careful!" She shone her phone at the ground by his feet.

There was a ring of stones there arranged in a neat circle. Precise and even, except where Tatsuya had kicked one of the stones. Definitely not the work of a bear.

"What is that?" She bent down, focusing on the ring of stones. The center was black and full of smeary ashes. "Is that a firepit?" She swung her phone around eagerly, and she caught sight of what might be other signs of human habitation. A heap of moldering wood. What looked for all the world like a rusty metal knife blade, although she didn't dare to touch it. "Did someone live here?"

Tatsuya hadn't spoken, she realized, since they'd discovered the cave.

"Tatsuya?"

"Someone lived here," he agreed. His voice was like the rusty creak of an old gate. "An ogre lived here."

"That's..."

"Can't you tell? Can't you feel it?" he insisted.

It was like there was an unreality field around him, distorting what she knew to be true, replacing it with this shared delusion. He believed it. Grandmother believed it.

Inoue Enryō had been wrong, she thought. The mosquito bite at the base of her neck itched. Her wet skirt clung to her legs. She was suddenly aware that there was still blood welling up from her scraped knee. Ogres chewing on girl's naked thighs...

There was a broad flat rock beside the firepit. Tatsuya sat heavily on it and rested his elbows on his knees. He looked steadily up at her—looking straight at her for the first time.

"Let's go back outside," she suggested.

He didn't move, didn't speak. The sheer immovable weight of him compressed her chest, made it hard for her to breathe. He was going to stay here, she realized. He was going to stay in the cave. Because he believed it was where he belonged.

Hitomi knelt on the hard floor of the cave, on the other side of the firepit from Tatsuya. Where there would have been a fire, long ago. She set her phone on the ground between them, the weak blue light from its screen barely illuminating his inscrutable ogre's face.

This wasn't what she was supposed to be doing in her fieldwork. She was supposed to listen and observe and analyze. Certainly not to intervene, to try to change the village or the people in it.

"I'm going to tell you a different story," she began. "Do you want to hear it?"

He nodded very slightly.

Long, long ago, in the Edo period or maybe earlier, in this village, in your family, there was a young woman who lived with her mother and father. She wanted to make things a little easier on her parents, so she would often go up into the mountains to gather brushwood to sell in the village.

Many people lived on mountains, back in those days. There were the villagers with their farms or their shops, of course. But deeper in the mountains, there were all sorts of other people. Travelers. Hermits. And hunters.

One day, while the young woman was gathering brushwood, she came upon a hunter. She was terrified of him at first. He was a huge man who didn't cut his hair or his beard. He wasn't like any of the men she knew from the village. And she was afraid of his arrows and knives.

But he spoke gently to her, even though he was such a big, wild man. And so the young woman started to look forward to seeing the hunter in the woods. They would share food together; he would give her bits of the meat he caught, and she would bring him little delicacies from the village, whatever she could spare.

Sometimes he even let her visit him in the cave where he lived. He was embarrassed, because he knew it wouldn't compare to her home in the village, but she was happy there. Because she could be alone with him.

She never told her parents about him. He wasn't the sort of man she was supposed to be seeing. She was the village beauty, and she knew she was supposed to marry a village boy. Not the hunter, who came down from the mountain once in a while to sell his catch, but belonged outside the village.

And one day, the young woman decided to stay on the mountain with the hunter. The villagers would never accept him as her husband, so she had no other choice. So, for a time, they lived together in his cave in perfect happiness as man and wife.

They might have spent their whole lives on the mountain together, but before too long, the young woman was with child. Although she was delighted to carry the hunter's child, she realized that she could not raise a child alone in the hunter's cave. Her baby would be better off in the village, with a roof over its head, and its grandparents and neighbors to help care for it. So she reluctantly parted from her husband and returned to the village to give birth.

The young woman gave birth to a son who grew up to be just as strong and bold as his father, the hunter. She was always wonderfully proud of him, but he was different from all the other children in the village. And because he was different, and his children were different, and his children's children were different, the villagers began to make up stories about the family. The same way we make up stories about anyone who is different.

The young woman never told her story to anyone, not even her son, so it was forgotten, and the villagers' lie was remembered instead. But you and I know the truth.

∗

Hitomi wasn't an experienced storyteller like Grandmother. But she had practice, at least, in retelling her own story. And she had tried her best.

"You just made that up," Tatsuya pointed out. His eyes shone in the dark.

"Your grandmother isn't the only one who can tell stories. You can have your own story, too. Especially about yourself."

Hitomi understood, finally, why she had chosen a degree in folklore. Not just because it was deliciously impractical, but to study the stories we tell ourselves about ourselves. It was just what she had needed at a time when she had to rewrite herself. And no one needed a different story more desperately than Tatsuya.

He sat without speaking for a long time, but she could wait. She felt the ringing silence of the cave, the great weight of the mountain above and around them. Her injured knee throbbed, her legs cramped, and her phone ran out of battery.

"You could come to Tokyo one day," she said. Her voice echoed strangely in the cave. "I'd show you around. It's full of people, and you might hate it... but sometimes it's good to experience something new."

"Maybe," he conceded roughly. "One day." She tried to imagine him in Tokyo, hunching to fit through the train doors on the Yamanote line, towering above the press of people in the Shibuya scramble... It wasn't impossible.

The muffled sound of raindrops from outside the cave slowed. Hitomi stood, her legs shaking from kneeling on the floor of the cave, and peeked outside. The light hurt her eyes.

"The rain has stopped. Do you want to go home?" she asked. Standing there in the mouth of the cave, she offered him her hand and held her breath.

The massive shadow of Tatsuya was unmoving inside the dark cave. She couldn't see his face, couldn't tell what he was thinking. The light from outside barely filtered through the narrow entrance of the cave, cast weird shadows behind him. For a moment his form blurred; she saw his red face, his horns, his cruel fangs. But then they were gone.

When he stood, he was a person like anyone else: huge and ugly and gentle and human.

Tatsuya grabbed her hand and let her pull him out of the cave.

See Felicity Drake's story "Kozuna, the Ogre's Child" online at Metaphorosis.
If you liked it, leave a comment. Authors love that!
Remember to subscribe to our e-mail updates so you'll know when new stories are posted.

About the story

I'm a little embarrassed to admit how personal this story is. It's woven together from my own experiences, people I've met, places I've been, and stories I've read.

"Kozuna, the Ogre's Child" is the name of a real Japanese folktale. (Grandmother's version of the story is fairly similar to those you'll find in collections of Japanese folklore.) The first time I heard it, I felt awful for poor Kozuna, the half-ogre boy. It wasn't his fault that he had ogre blood, and the story gave him no chance for redemption or a happy ending.

The setting is inspired by Gokayama: a UNESCO world heritage site in Toyama Prefecture, and a unique, beautiful place with a thriving tourist trade. (And yes, the tofu really is life-changingly delicious!) For the setting of the story, I imagined a shadow twin of the real Gokayama, a neighboring village without the UNESCO stamp of approval and the tourist income it brings.

The picture scroll that Hitomi thinks about, the one with ogres banqueting on human flesh and blood, is *Shuten dōji emaki*. The version I had in mind can be viewed online, thanks to the National Diet Library's digital collection (http://dl.ndl.go.jp/info:ndljp/pid/1287887?tocOpened=1).

If the folklore of the mountains of Japan captures your imagination, I would strongly recommend Yanagita Kunio's *The Legends of Tono* (translated by Ronald A. Morse). It is a classic of folklore studies and a gateway into another world.

A question for the author

Q: What's your favorite type of pie?

A: Can't go wrong with a classic apple pie. I recommend adding raisins!

About the author

Felicity Drake is a writer based in New York. She writes fiction and interactive fiction.

www.felicitydrake.com, @DrakeFelicity

Magical Whistleblower Tells All

Michael Sherrin

August 19

FLYING MAN CLAIMS MAGIC IS REAL

London – Magic exists, says Thaddeus Seams, 37. Mr. Seams claims to be a wizard belonging to a secret society with real magical abilities. Monday morning, Mr. Seams landed in Trafalgar Square, dressed in velvet robes and holding an alleged magic wand.

"It looked like real magic," said Daisey Patricks, 53, who was present when Mr. Seams arrived. "He was flying above our heads, then landed in the middle of the street."

Several witnesses reported the man projecting his voice across the square without a microphone or other form of amplification.

Police escorted Mr. Seams into a car. Both the police department and Downing Street declined to comment until they had investigated the claims.

A representative of the British Magical Society issued a statement saying Mr. Seams has never been a member and that their organization has never claimed magic is real.

August 22
WORLD'S FIRST WIZARD
TAKES MANHATTAN

New York City – Self-proclaimed wizard, Thaddeus Seams, held a press conference today at the Waldorf Astoria to perform his magic for invited members of the press.

Mr. Seams began his remarks by saying he represented a hidden society of conjurers who lived around the world, using magic in secret, attending special schools and operating their own government, which set rules about how magic should be used. He added that by revealing magic to the world, he was breaking the laws of his society.

Mr. Seams went on to demonstrate several spells. With a few waves of his wand and speaking unidentifiable words, he repaired a broken chair, mended a tear in a dress, and healed an audience member's broken arm.

A hotel spokesperson said Mr. Seams tried to pay for a suite and use of the ballroom with several gold coins featuring names and words not recognized as any known language. An independent appraiser offered to pay the hotel on behalf of Mr. Seams in exchange for the coins, though he would not comment on their value.

September 4

MR. WIZARD GOES TO WASHINGTON

Washington, D.C. – Congress held hearings Tuesday afternoon to investigate the claims of whistleblower, Thaddeus Seams, that a secret, magic society exists. Mr. Seams insists that there are thousands of wizards like him hiding in the world, operating a shadow government and economy.

Scientists, occult experts, and religious leaders are also scheduled to testify over two days of hearings about the potential existence of magic.

September 4
> TESTIMONY OF THADDEUS SEAMS
> (Excerpt)

Congressman Harris – What was your profession in this magical world, Mr. Seams?

Seams – I work in the Office of Teleportation and Transportation as a deconstruction analyst.

Harris – Can you explain what that role entails?

Seams – I monitor teleportation traffic around the world to ensure conjurers don't appear on top of one another, considering it's difficult to see where you're going when you're already there.

[Laughter from chambers]

Harris – You mean you can use magic to teleport? How does that work?

Seams – It just works, sir. It's magic.

Congresswoman Brown – You mean to say your society can teleport instantaneously across cities?

Seams – A strong conjurer can teleport across countries, sometimes continents with the right channeling.

Brown – Can you explain why you've chosen to keep this technology secret?

Seams – It's not technology. And it wasn't my choice to keep it secret. I think magic should be –

Brown – How long has your society had the ability to teleport?

Seams – Thousands of years, I believe.

Brown – Do you realize the damage caused by keeping this a secret? Teleportation could have solved climate change. No more emissions from cars or planes.

Seams – Yes, madam, I realize that. It's part of why I decided to come forward.

Brown – Though you admit to keeping this a secret for years yourself.

Seams – [Drinks water, refills it with his wand] Yes. There's a great deal of magic that's not being utilized to its fullest. I've tried speaking to the leadership in the conjuring community about engaging open relations with the mundane world, but I was rebuffed.

They believe magic is too powerful to
share. I say that is precisely the reason
we should share it.

Brown – Why now, Mr. Seams? What
made you come forward as you have?

Seams – To save the world, of course.

September 9

WIZARD CASTS SPELL ON SCIENTISTS

Chicago – A team of scientists met with
the wizard Thaddeus Seams in Hyde Park
on Monday to examine his alleged magical
abilities and artifacts.

Scientists familiar with the meeting
described the wizard as friendly and eager
to share his knowledge.

Several noted particular interest in his
bag, which was leather and about the size
of a laptop case. According to Mr. Seams,
the bag contained a library of more than
three thousand books and specimens of
thought-to-be make-believe creatures.

Dr. James Goldhaber was in
attendance and said he saw some of the
most amazing things in his career. "I don't
know how he did it, but he pulled a
jackalope from his bag. The jackalope was
bigger than the bag."

"This bag either disproves core tenets of physics," said Dr. Florence Manning, a professor of theoretical physics at the University of Chicago, "or it reveals that other spatial dimensions not only exist, but may be accessible if we can turn this 'magic' into functional technology. The applications could be endless."

September 21
RELIGIOUS LEADERS CONCERNED ABOUT MAGIC

Geneva – Representatives from world religions convened to discuss the implications of magic on theology and society.

Dr. Swati Tharoor, author of three books on Hinduism, said during her opening keynote, "Miracles have been a part of almost every religion, and now we have the chance to see these miracles for ourselves. My question is, why now?"

Rev. Kurt Succow, after a panel discussing the subject of miracles, said in an interview, "For the first time in my life, I find myself turning toward science rather than faith for answers."

While many were optimistic about the good magic could bring to poor and suffering people, some dismissed it as a fraud no different from sham preachers hawking fake cures.

Leaflets calling the wizard Thaddeus Seams the Anti-Christ, were spread among the attendees. Police say they have no suspects as to who created the leaflets.

Over a phone interview, Mr. Seams addressed his and the conjuring community's views on religion saying, "Much as in the mundane world, there are a variety of perspectives among my people, though generally gods are not part of the conversation."

September 23
U.N. RESOLUTION DEMANDS MAGIC BE ACCESSIBLE TO ALL COUNTRIES

Beijing – China proposed a U.N. resolution, with more than fifty sponsors, to include representatives from all interested countries in the investigation of magic's legitimacy.

In a statement, President Jiang Biwu criticized the wizard Thaddeus Seams for spending all his time in the United States, ignoring the interests of the rest of the world, writing, "It is in the interest of China and all other countries to know about any secret societies within their borders. Mr. Seams must provide his knowledge to the global community."

Algerian Prime Minister Mouloud Sifi spoke in support of the resolution, saying, "Our countries must pay for drugs to save our lives, for patents to build our infrastructure, for companies to exploit our natural resources. Magic may be the first truly democratized resource, and its access should not be restricted."

In a letter brought by a pigeon, Mr. Seams wrote in response to our request for comment, "The Conjuring Community is as diverse as the world it's hidden within. I intend to share my knowledge of magic as widely as I can, though I am not a diplomat nor am I practiced in world affairs. I ask for patience as I try to learn as much about you as you learn about me."

September 25
INTERVIEW WITH SEAMS ON KATHY MARTIN LIVE

Kathy Martin – I'd like to welcome my first
    guest, the most interesting man in the
    world, the wizard, Thaddeus Seams.
[Applause]
Martin – Thank you for joining us.
Seams – Thank you for having me.
Martin – You've impressed a lot of people
    with your abilities. You say you want to
    save the world. How do you plan to do
    that?
Seams – My hope is that by my coming
    forward about magic, the conjuring
    community will recognize that staying
    secret benefits no one, and instead
    choose to help solve the big problems
    in the world. There are wizards with
    powers well beyond my own, and they
    could accomplish a great deal.
Martin – Are you concerned that no one
    has come forward to verify your claims
    of a secret society? How do you explain
    that?
Seams – There is a lot of misinformation
    about the mundane world in our
    community. We have our own
    newspapers, so our impressions are
    filtered and uninformed.
Martin – You mean there's no freedom of
    the press?

Seams – No, that's not what I mean. We have reporters, but they tend to cover the conjuring community rather than regular people. They say it's what viewers want.

Martin – Do they see themselves as better than us?

Seams – Unfortunately, some do.

Martin – Do you, Mr. Seams? Is this how you're planning to save us?

Seams – No, not at all. I just want to help. We're all people, regardless of our abilities. We should all share the resources we have available.

Martin – But why has no wizard come forward before?

Seams – It's illegal to reveal magic to non-conjurers.

Martin – So you've broken the law.

Seams – I have. I think the law is wrong and unfair. Everyone should have access to the benefits of magic, not just the conjuring community.

Martin – If magic is so powerful, how is there no other evidence of it?

Seams – There have been incidents. Often, it's an honest mistake – a spell is cast just as a witness passes by. There's a department that specializes in memory spells to deal with these accidents.

Martin – You mean mind control?

Seams – Oh no, this is completely different than mind control.

Martin – So you're confirming mind control exists.

Seams – Well, yes, but...

Martin – Mr. Seams, how do we know you haven't been using mind control on us?

Seams – I'm not that powerful. It takes an incredibly powerful...

Martin – Mr. Seams, should we be concerned that magic is a threat to our society?

Seams – No, not at all. Magic is a good thing.

Martin – But you said there are some wizards who think themselves better than us.

Seams – There have been evil wizards in the past, but we've been able to contain the damage...

Martin – Mr. Seams, how do we know you're one of the good ones?

September 26
        BACKLASH AGAINST WIZARD
              LEADS TO RIOT

New York City – A protest took place Wednesday night outside the Waldorf Astoria where wizard Thaddeus Seams has been staying. After a contentious interview on Kathy Martin Live, Mr. Seams has been subjected to criticism for potential abuse of his magical abilities, including mind control and wiping memories.

Daniel Rawlins, one of the protestors, said, "We don't let just anyone have nuclear weapons or tanks. How do we know what this wizard is doing to us?"

Assemblywoman Georgia Keegan spoke to the almost 500 protestors, saying only dictators and fascists hoard power for themselves. "This wizard is living in his ivory tower and doesn't have to worry about putting food on the table or keeping his kids clothed. He can just cast a spell."

October 1

DOCTORS DEMAND ACCESS TO
MAGICAL HEALING TO SAVE LIVES

Kinshasa – Dr. Louisa Famba said in an interview that she had requested wizard Thaddeus Seams use magic to address the recent outbreak of Ebola in three cities in the Democratic Republic of the Congo. There have been at least twelve new cases over the past three days, with more than 3,000 cases this year and more than 2,000 deaths. Dr. Famba said this outbreak was taxing what few healthcare resources her country has, and that the virus' communicability made it almost impossible to eradicate. "Magic might be cheaper and more effective than a vaccine," Dr. Famba said. "Vaccines cost millions to research and distribute. Magic appears to only require a wand."

Mr. Seams previously demonstrated the ability to heal broken bones more effectively than current medical science. In testimony to Congress, Mr. Seams further claimed magic could cure any non-magical disease.

"From malaria to HIV to Ebola," Dr. Famba said, "we are at the epicenter of the worst epidemic since the 1918 Spanish Flu. If magic can save lives, why won't he use his power to do so?"

Dr. Ismail Hassan, a representative with the World Health Organization, said if magic's health properties are found to be safe and effective, many diseases and chronic issues could become curable, saving an estimated 25 million lives per year.

Mr. Seams declined to comment.

October 10
STATEMENT FROM U.N. SECRETARY-GENERAL ADDRESSING THREAT OF MAGIC

Following are U.N. Secretary-General Aamir Wasim's remarks to the Security Council meeting on security and trade with the Conjuring Community.

Less than two months ago, we believed the greatest threats to humanity were made by science. I did not believe magic existed and remain skeptical of such claims. While Mr. Seams has performed miracles I cannot explain through science or God, the locations he provided as the sites of secret schools and shopping centers have not been found by satellite or on-the-ground inspections. That said, there is reason to err on the side of belief, balancing the benefits and risks.

If magic exists, it has the potential to do more good in this world than electricity, running water, and penicillin combined. It also could destabilize our economies, destroy faith in our leaders, and subject us to dangers we cannot fathom.

If these wizards can control our minds, could we stop them from launching nuclear weapons? Could they use magic to replicate our currency, causing havoc in our economies? What if they decide our way of life, our religions, or use of resources, infringe on their magical territory?

I urge the Security Council to stand with me in denouncing the Conjuring Community for hiding their natural resource and refusing to engage in diplomatic relations with their countrymen and neighbors. If the Conjuring Community do not reveal themselves, the Security Council should consider escalating the issue as a direct threat on the well-being of the world.

October 12
SELECTION OF SOCIAL MEDIA POSTS
FROM MORNING OF OCTOBER 12
Traffic is not moving on#CharingCross.
WTF? – @mraccountant87 – 0903

Is anyone else's Google Maps having trouble connecting? I'm in #LeicesterSq – @bellattahere – 0904

What the hell is Casting Road? I don't recognize this street at all. – @britstone3456 – 0904

Does anyone recognize this building in #LeicesterSq? Photo attached – @downtondorthy – 0906

Someone moved the Burger King to put in a townhouse! #LeicesterSq – @killzme76 – 0907

Transcript from video upload by @abbyyouknow01:

"Hey, my followers, Abby You Know here in Leicester Sq. where things are getting weird. Like, roads have changed and the buildings have all moved. Everyone is running around all confused and weirded out.

"So this building that's now in the middle of all the tourist shops is like an old castle or something. It's all stone and tall but crooked and weird. Someone's coming out. It's an old lady. She's got cool robes on. Girl's got some fashion. Holy shit, she has a wand. She's lifting it up. Can you hear her? She's saying she's the Chief Conjurer.

"What's a Chief Conjurer?"

October 15

EYE-WITNESS ACCOUNT OF THE
FIRST MAGICAL SUMMIT

This is Cooper Wolf in Paris, reporting for the Prize News Network at the first summit between world leaders and the Conjuring Community. There are more than three hundred people in attendance, including twelve wizards.

Thaddeus Seams, the man who started all this by blowing the whistle on magic, is also here.

Seams is seated near the central dais to the side. I must say, he looks a bit pale.

The Chief Conjurer, Abigail Lyre, is taking her seat between the Secretary-General and the French president who's hosting this gathering. Mrs. Lyre seems vibrant and bright, though she needed help stepping onto the dais.

President Francois is welcoming everyone and proclaims this a great day in the history of humanity, saying we're venturing down a new road of discovery and development.

The Secretary-General is standing now and saying he looks forward to peaceful relations with the conjurers and hopes they can share their great abilities to rid the world of illness and famine and turn back the damage of climate change.

The Chief Conjurer is taking her turn. She stands slowly, resting a hand on the president's shoulder.

[Audio from Mrs. Lyre's microphone]

"Thank you, President Francois and Mr. Secretary. We are honored to be your guests, and though this may not be under the circumstances we would have chosen, we are appreciative of the opportunity.

"Magic has been around for millennia, and it has been kept secret all that time. Pain and strife have existed for even longer, and magic is no salve. The purpose of keeping magic restricted was to allow human development without a crutch. You have created light bulbs and airplanes, all to compensate for a lack of magical abilities. This is something that should be admired and respected."

[Mrs. Lyre pauses and draws her wand from her sleeve]

"However, it is not our fault that you have not managed to use your technology to solve your greatest problems. You allow poverty to exist even though there is enough wealth to share. You allow families to starve even though there is an abundance of food. You fight over oil, even though the substance is destroying this planet.

"This is why we chose to hide – because we could not help you solve your own problems. It should be your responsibility to fix them.

"But that option is no longer available to us, thanks to the irresponsible ramblings of a rogue actor.

"While in isolated incidents, we have managed to extract memories of our existence, that will not work anymore, as the knowledge has now spread too wide. Your veiled threats against our safety and security required us to address this head on. We have decided the best course of action would be for the Conjurer Council to take over governance of the entire populous, effective immediately."

[End audio from microphone]

Cooper Wolf reporting. Everyone has exploded in anger. People are leaping onto their chairs and yelling at the Chief Conjurer. I will do my best to continue reporting, though it is impossible to hear what anyone is saying through the pandemonium.

It looks as if President Francois is trying to reason with the Chief Conjurer, but she is just looking at the crowd with a smile.

[Sound from stage cuts out]

The room just went completely silent, though the representatives still look like they're shouting. I'm far in the back and don't seem to have been affected. It was like the air was sucked out. The Chief Conjurer has her wand out. I think she just cast a spell on everyone. Hopefully my feed is still transmitting. People are returning to their seats.

[Audio from Mrs. Lyre's microphone]

"As you can see, you cannot govern yourselves. You need someone to coddle you, silence you. This is a simple spell so we can discuss the future, together, calmly. I hope you appreciate that we do this not by choice, but by circumstance. We will cure your diseases and feed your hungry, and we ask nothing in return. Just the chance to bring the world together, for the first time. And for this, we have Thaddeus Seams to thank."

[End audio from microphone]

The Chief Conjurer has turned to Seams, who is still seated with his hands covering his face. She's clapping, and the whole room is starting to as well. Apparently, so am I. We're all clapping.

October 14
EDITORIAL: WORLD THANKS CONJURING COMMUNITY

New York City – Celebrations will be taking place around the world tomorrow on the first Magic Day, in honor of the Conjuring Community and their role in saving the world. Climate change is being reversed. Disease, war, crime, and famine are almost non-existent because of magic spells.

No more are nations part of the first world or the third world. There is no wealth and no poverty. Everyone is happy thanks to magic making everything wonderful.

Part of the celebrations are in dedication to Thaddeus Seams, the man responsible for bringing about this Golden Age. Though Mr. Seams hasn't been seen since the Paris Summit when world leaders begged the Conjuring Council to take over governance, his contributions for diplomatically bringing these worlds together are worthy of praise.

The world is a better place thanks to the wisdom and generosity of the Conjuring Community. Their continued guidance will bring a new age of prosperity and peace, and it is our unquestioning trust in them that will bring that future to today.

EXCERPT FROM "THE PERSONAL PENNED TREATISE OF MR. THADDEUS SEAMS"

Magic is too powerful to be trusted. Its uses are too secret, its guardians too few.

I never thought I would last this long. I expected the Community to try to stop me before I could demonstrate magic beyond what spells could wash away. Maybe they knew I had contingencies planned. I'm not the most powerful conjurer, but I prepared.

My autoscribtor is documenting everything I did and said and is manifesting copies in secret locations around the world. Should the pen ever stop writing, these copies will be sent to every newspaper and world leader. It would mean I'm no longer able to able to represent magic myself.

It won't be long until they attempt to hide magic again. Knowledge is most powerful when rare, and knowledge of magic is the most powerful of all.

Yet it is the willingness of people to forget that will forever impress me, even when remembering should be so much easier.

Memories are a form of energy and energy cannot be destroyed. But no one seems willing to put the effort into digging deep enough to find what's hidden. When magic has been exposed before, often by accident, the event is wiped and the memory written off as a dream or something from a movie or book. The memory remains, locked away, hidden within a mind uninterested in what isn't readily available.

I know a written recitation will not serve as an adequate replacement for seeing magic in-person, but I hope it will help awaken what has been lost.

If what I say sounds bizarre or make believe, push past that assumption. It will feel uncomfortable. Maybe you'll even laugh at the consideration that what I've said is true. But keep pushing. Recall the days as I described them, consider the details I offered, and probe yourself for memories equal in detail. The more you push, the more the fog will thicken, making it easier to look the other way and ignore the injustice done to you.

The magicians of your world understand that magic is all about sleight of hand. While they use distraction and mirrors for their illusions, real magic finds value in similarly being ignored. If you knew the influence it had over your decisions, the power it had over your lives, your choices would no longer be your own. Ignorance allows magic to reign without impediment.

I fear there will not be another after me willing to take this risk should I fail. The decision to betray my people did not come easily. Had my life taken a slightly different course, it is possible my choice would have been different. Bravery was never my strong suit. Even with my magical abilities, I've spent my life toiling away at a desk in a room without a window, and all to make magic a bit more efficient. It was like rearranging grains of sand to make for a more pleasant beach.

I hope this document helps break through the fog and leads to a better, more equal world. This may be my final act. There is no way to know if I've succeeded. It is up to you who read this to believe that what I say is the truth and to refuse being blinded from what is hiding in plain sight.

Disclaimer: This is a work of fiction. Any resemblance to actual persons or memories is purely coincidental and should be ignored.

"See Michael Sherrin's story "Magic Whistleblower Tells All" online at Metaphorosis. If you liked it, leave a comment. Authors love that!
Remember to subscribe to our e-mail updates so you'll know when new stories are posted."

About the story

The inspirations for "Magical Whistleblower Tells All" are worn on its sleeve, from Harry Potter to Buffy to the many other secret magical world stories. I love many of these, though I've always found the reasoning to keep magic or monsters or technology a secret lacking. Often, I feel, the secrecy is meant to allow the suspension of disbelief, that this world could exist in reality (much like the many of us eagerly awaiting Hogwarts invitations).

This story challenges the premise that keeping power secret is somehow a good thing. I aimed to develop reasoning for the secrecy, giving a different point of view to this common trope, and then unmask it for all harm it does, ideally for the purpose of relating it to our real world restrictions — income inequality, patented drugs, DRMed information — all ways useful tools are restricted from many who would value them.

A question for the author

Q: Where do you write?

A: I write in my home office, which is part of a finished basement, where I'm surrounded by shelves of my 2,000+ action figures. These serve as both inspiration and distraction.

Depending on my mood, I'll write at my desktop, which is better for long drafting and research (multiple screens, again, both helpful and harmful), or on my laptop on my recliner, which lets me focus just on the text (better for editing) or napping.

I find myself the most productive late at night. I can spend the whole day "working," yet the hours between 11pm — 1am will be more productive than the many hours worked before.

About the author

Michael Sherrin developed his preference for fiction when he learned reality didn't include a real Spider-Man. He has an MBA from the Kellogg School of Management, where he learned to write riveting Excel formulas, though the solutions were often predictable. By day, he works with complex analytical algorithms, and by night he works on short stories and his novel. Michael lives outside Boston with his husband, dog, and several thousand action figures.

www.prodigeek.com, @prodigeek

Choice

Tomas Marcantonio

The giant apartment complex was unfinished, like almost everything else in Pyongyang. It loomed over the city, a grey, oval-shaped mass rising like a fungal growth on the bank of the Taedong River, swarming with half-lived lives. The western side was wall-less, held together with sagging electrical wires and iron bones stripped of their skin. Multitudes of drones hovered outside windows, transporting deliveries or simply spying, like mechanical wasps searching for a nectar that no longer existed.

The air inside the elevator was thick and sour, with a pervading stench of rotten eggs. A dead rat lay in one corner, the toes of its pink feet bent pathetically into its body. Sora couldn't drag her eyes from it as they ascended, the elevator shuddering and groaning at intervals.

"I hate this city," Gyuri said, digging her hands into the pockets of her trench coat. "Reunification was the worst thing that could've happened to this damn country." She looked to her superior. "I keep forgetting. You voted for it, didn't you?"

Sora kept her eyes on the dead creature next to Gyuri's foot. "We thought it was the most humane thing to do," she said carefully. They were passing the eightieth floor and she felt the pressure building in her ears; she swallowed to equalise it.

"Yeah, well maybe sometimes it's best just to cut the dead weight loose. Imagine how the south would look now if we hadn't blown our money on this wasteland."

Sora said nothing. Gyuri was too young to remember how it was; she never saw the horrors that came with the first nuclear missiles. The war was over as soon as it had begun.

When the doors jerked open on the hundred and twelfth floor, Gyuri used her foot to drag the rat corpse into the dark corridor.

"Now we won't have to look at it on the way down," she said, rolling it onto its back.

The corridor was low-ceilinged and narrow, flanked by steel apartment doors. Black bags of waste were courted by swarms of flies, and a communal bathroom leaked yellow light and a fetid smell. Sora led the way, stopping at the final door on the right.

"This one," she said.

Gyuri checked the engraved number and knocked. A moment later the door opened inwards just a fraction, enough to reveal a suspicious eye and a silver chain. A TV was blaring behind it.

"What do you want?"

Sora flashed her badge. "Yoo Sora," she said, "Seoul National Detective Agency. This is my partner, Kwon Gyuri. We're looking for Jeong Hoon."

"That's me."

"In that case we'd like to speak to you."

The eye blinked twice quickly. The door closed and the women heard the scratching sound of the latch being removed. When the door opened again, Jeong Hoon stood back to let them inside.

The room was little more than a shoebox. The walls were grey concrete, decorated only by blotches of blood forming purple halos around the flattened, mangled bodies of mosquitoes. A mattress was folded in one corner, a pile of clothes strewn on top. An ancient Samsung TV took up a quarter of the room. Jeong Hoon shoved his clothes to one side and sat cross-legged on the mattress, gesturing for the women to take seats on the lino floor.

Sora tried not to inhale through her nose; the window was closed, and Sora guessed from the intense smell of body odour that it had been closed for a long time.

"Would you mind turning the TV off?"

Hoon furrowed his brows briefly before reaching for the bulky remote at his side. He pointed it at the screen, pausing with his finger over the power button. A man in a white coat was describing the benefits of a new respirator; a map behind him showed a yellow cloud moving from the great landmass of China to the Korean peninsula. Hoon turned off the TV and a sudden, heavy silence filled the room.

"What's this about?" Hoon asked.

The window allowed a shaft of dusk light to fall across his coarse-looking crew cut. He had a wide nose and a prominent forehead, and one of his ears stuck out more than the other.

"Have you ever heard of a Seoul-based company from the 2030s that went by the name of Choice?" Sora asked.

Hoon shook his head.

"Choice was one of several private companies that performed surgical abortions in the thirties and forties," Sora went on. "However, the staff of Choice didn't believe in abortions at all; in fact, they were staunchly pro-life."

Hoon watched her without expression.

"In the years following reunification, birth rates on the peninsula were lower than ever, and one of Choice's goals was to find a solution to the rapidly ageing population of the New Republic. They were sponsored by certain high-ranking officials to use artificial wombs to keep aborted foetuses alive, all without the mother's knowledge. Once the babies reached the end of their gestation period, they were taken to orphanages and eventually fostered around the country, often to families here in the north, where birth rates were lowest."

Hoon scratched behind his ear. Gyuri watched him intently, drumming her fingers lightly on the floor.

"Of course," Sora said, "once these activities were exposed years later, Choice was shut down and everyone involved was arrested, with many facing lengthy prison sentences."

Hoon shrugged. "And what does all that have to do with me?"

Sora tucked her bob behind her ears and glanced at her partner.

"How was your relationship with Mr. and Mrs. Jeong?" Gyuri asked. "The people who brought you up?"

It was the first time the younger woman had spoken and Hoon's eyes lingered on her silky black hair, then on her pale, youthful face. It was a face that could have been pretty, the men in the office often reminded her, if it hadn't worn a perpetually disgruntled expression.

Hoon shrugged again. "They were just parents. They left me enough money to get by after they died."

"They weren't your real parents, Hoon, that's what we're trying to tell you."

Sora winced inwardly, but was grateful for her partner's candor.

"So what?" Hoon said, fingering the lobe of his protruding ear, "You're telling me I was one of these aborted babies? I was born in a lab?"

Sora nodded slowly. "At fifteen weeks you were transferred to a sophisticated artificial womb, where you were provided with the necessary nutrients and conditions to keep you alive."

Hoon pulled himself slowly to his feet and turned to the window. Sora and Gyuri exchanged a glance behind his back. Gyuri reached questioningly for the stun gun on her belt, but Sora shook her head.

"So are you hooking me up with my real parents or something?" Hoon asked, turning around. "Is that what this is?"

"You saw our badges, Hoon," Gyuri said. "We're not some charity. Setting you up for a reunion isn't our priority."

Hoon fixed the young woman with a penetrating stare. "Then what is your priority?"

Sora raised a hand to quiet her partner. "The aborted babies," she began falteringly. "At first they appeared to show no signs of ill-adjustment. At a young age they were often quieter, more detached, but that's not uncommon in adopted children anyway. However, recent studies have revealed changes, usually when the subjects reach their mid-to-late teens. On average, subjects of the Choice births show significantly lower levels of empathy than natural-born people of the same age. They are also far more likely to commit crimes — violent crimes." Sora watched for the boy's reaction. "You've had a few run-ins with the law, haven't you, Hoon?"

"I've never killed anyone."

"No, we know you haven't," Sora said.

"You might be a danger to society," Gyuri cut in. Sora closed her eyes and pinched the bridge of her nose. "That's what we're trying to tell you, all right? Sooner or later all the subjects start going off the rails, and we're going to put you somewhere safe and run some tests until we're sure you're not going to go the same way. Got it?"

Sora took a deep breath. "We believe these aspects of your personality may have been due to the supplements you were given in the artificial womb."

"Yeah," Gyuri said, "and the fact that you spent more than half your gestation period inside a fish tank instead of the body of a loving mother."

For a moment Hoon said nothing. He stared at Gyuri before turning back to the window.

"Gyuri," Sora said. "Would you mind waiting outside?"

Gyuri muttered something as she stood and exited, closing the door forcibly behind her.

For a moment Sora sat in silence, watching the back of Hoon's head.

"Are they still alive?" he asked.

"Who?"

"My parents. My real parents. Are they still alive?"

Sora peered at the flexible display strapped to her forearm. She swiped through the case files and skimmed the brief on Hoon's parents. "Your mother is alive, yes. In Pyongyang, as it happens. According to the documents she signed at the time of the abortion, she didn't know the identity of your father. She cited the reason for the abortion as—"

"Can I see her?"

"Our job is to take you directly to the institution in Seoul for tests," Sora said. "It's a safe environm—"

"I just want to see her once," Hoon said, and for the first time Sora heard a note of anxiety in his voice. "Once, before I go. Please. I want to see my mother."

Sora looked searchingly into the young man's eyes. None of the subjects had shown such interest in their birth parents before. Perhaps, she thought, glancing over her shoulder at the door, this was the subject she had been waiting for all these months.

"The chief is going to be pissed if he finds out," Gyuri said.

"Then he won't find out," Sora said.

The Taedong Ferry chugged south-westerly through the city. The river was clogged with rusted tankers and smaller fishing boats cushioned between islands of floating garbage. Shanty houses clung to the riverbanks like layers of plaque on rotten teeth. They were mostly empty now; millions had fled to Seoul after the treaty and now Pyongyang festered, half in squalor, half forgotten.

"It won't take long," Sora said, absently scanning the deserted hovels.

Gyuri pulled her dust mask down over her chin and lit up a cigarette, blowing a cloud of smoke into the misty evening air.

"You always want to give them a chance," she said, inspecting the cigarette between her fingers. "Like one of them's going to turn up with a dumb smile and tell you it's all a mistake, that there's nothing wrong with them."

Sora stared across deck at Hoon, sat on a bench out of earshot, his shoulders hunched.

"They're bad eggs, boss," Gyuri went on. "You can see it just looking at them. The only surprise is how long it took for the gov to give us the green light to round them all up."

Sora turned back to the water, leaning on the railings.

"You don't believe in it, do you?" Gyuri asked. "Abortion."

Sora sighed. "There are only two outcomes of an unwanted pregnancy, and they're both as tragic as each other. The only thing that matters is that the mother makes the decision. That's why Choice was so deplorable; they stole that right from those women.

"When you look into their eyes, Gyuri," she added, "don't you see the tragedy of it all? Their mothers never meant for them to be born. They were so close to never existing. The way Hoon looked when he asked about his mother. I don't know, maybe they don't all have to turn out like we expect. Maybe there's hope for them."

Gyuri dropped her cigarette to the floor and crushed it under her shoe.

"Still," she said, replacing her dust mask, "you'll be in deep shit if they find out. The mother knows we're on the way?"

"She's one of the minority; most of them didn't want to know when the news broke. Imagine finding out that the child you aborted had lived on."

Gyuri shrugged and brushed her hair behind one ear as the ferry approached the city centre. Skyscrapers pierced the sky around the crumbling remains of Juche Tower, some crowned with redundant cranes, others dotted with amber windows, the refuge of after-hours office workers desperately shackling themselves to their jobs. The network of back-alleys behind the dock bustled with street food smoke and the sorry exhausts of ancient scooters.

"Let's get this done quick, then," Gyuri said. "Before we're both out of a job."

The boarding house was in a dilapidated building above a rowdy bar that served home-brewed makgeolli and greasy pajeon. Sora led the way through the wood-paneled bar, stepping carefully past a red-faced man on the stairs, bald, wrinkled, and weeping quietly. Hoon's mother's room was at the end of the third-floor corridor, and she opened the door almost as soon as Sora's knuckles were done rapping on it. She was close to Sora's age, somewhere in her mid-thirties, though she looked older. Short and slight, she had a careworn, mousey expression and stringy hair that looked as though it hadn't been washed in days.

"Ms. Han," Sora said, flashing her badge. "Yoo Sora, we spoke on the phone."

Hoon's mother opened the door wider. "Is he here?"

"He is," Sora said, stepping aside to let Hoon through.

There was no great embrace as Hoon met his mother for the first time. Her eyes filled instantly with tears but she struggled to look directly at her son; she squinted and inclined her head slightly, as though he were an especially bright light. Sora and Gyuri followed them inside the modest room, uncluttered and half-clean.

"We can only give you five minutes," Sora said. "This is quite against regulations."

Hoon's mother nodded meekly, wringing her hands. She showed Sora and Gyuri onto the veranda and closed the door behind them. Sora pulled up her dust mask while the younger woman lit a cigarette.

"I don't want to hear it," Sora said.

"Whatever you say, boss. I just want to get this done and get back to Seoul. Who are we after next, anyway?"

Sora swiped at the monitor on her forearm and scanned the assignments folder.

"Well, who is it?"

Sora shook her head. She had known this day would come eventually, that she wouldn't be able to protect her partner forever.

"What's wrong? We're not in Pyongyang again, are we?"

"The system's down," Sora said, swiping the screen off. "I'll check again later."

Sora felt Gyuri's gaze on her as she regarded the smoky, blinking neon parade of Pyongyang's backstreets. A stray dog with three legs stopped outside the back door of the bar to piss on a pile of black sacks. Gyuri's eyes didn't leave Sora's face, and the stare seemed to gain in intensity with each passing second, like a branding iron being held to her cheek.

"Maybe we should give them a couple more minutes," Sora said, nodding over her shoulder.

Her partner, ignoring her, flicked her cigarette over the railing and pushed the door open into the apartment. Gyuri froze in the doorway, and Sora had to push her aside to see within.

Hoon was on his knees on the floor, his mother's head cradled in his hands, her hair between his fingers.

"Hoon," Sora whispered, "what have you done?"

Hoon dropped his mother's head to the floor, her body limp, her neck clearly broken.

"Eighteen years ago she tried to kill me," he said, his voice empty of emotion. "Now we're even."

He stood, wiping the palms of his hands against his legs. "I'm ready to go to the institution now," he said, holding his hands out before him.

Gyuri returned to the veranda to call headquarters. Sora found a bed sheet and spread it over the body of Hoon's mother. Hoon was sat next to her body, his hands cuffed and his legs crossed beneath him.

Sora knew she would lose her badge. She might even face manslaughter charges for gross negligence. It hardly mattered. She'd always known it would come to this, ever since she located Gyuri and recruited her.

"She doesn't know, does she?" Hoon said, looking up at her morosely.

"Who?" Sora asked.

"Your partner. How old is she?"

Sora stared down at the boy. "Eighteen, the same as you."

"You must have been young."

Sora said nothing. Hoon nodded.

"I'm guessing your bosses don't know about her, either."

Sora shook her head.

"You don't want her to turn out like me. I get it. But what if she doesn't? What if she lives a normal life? Are you going to tell her? That you had her aborted?"

"I never imagined—" Sora began, but the words caught in her throat. "I thought you might be the one to change everything. That if you showed forgiveness, empathy, then Gyuri…"

The smile that formed on Hoon's lips was almost sinister in its simplicity.

"If it's really like you said, they'll take it into account, won't they? When they sentence me. The supplements you mentioned, the gestation tanks. That's the reason, isn't it, for everything in here?" He tapped his temple with a finger. "I mean, it's not me. It wasn't my choice."

Sora considered him. No, it wasn't his choice. It wasn't his mother's choice, either.

Hoon gazed at his cuffed hands, his palms open, as though trying to measure something. "Fifteen weeks," he said, almost to himself. "Is there a heartbeat at fifteen weeks?"

Sora stared at the space between his hands and nodded.

Gyuri re-entered the room. "They'll be here in ten." Kneeling, she pulled the sheet down and looked into the dead woman's face. "I wonder what she felt after they took the baby from her. I wonder if she ever regretted it."

"What does it matter?" Hoon said in his expressionless voice.

"She regretted it," Sora said, her voice shaking. "But what would you have done? Maybe she was poor, maybe she was too young. Maybe... maybe the father was a faceless man who forced himself on her. What would you have done, Gyuri, if it were you?"

Gyuri glanced at Hoon. He returned her gaze with his flat, impassive stare.

Gyuri rubbed her face and closed her eyes for what seemed like hours. When they opened, Sora expected to see tears gathered on her lashes, but there were none.

Gyuri stood gingerly, her eyes fixed on the face of Hoon's dead mother. She advanced slowly on Sora, who was blinking away tears, her hand hovering close to her belt.

"See Tomas Marcantonio's story "Choice" online at Metaphorosis.
If you liked it, leave a comment. Authors love that!
Remember to subscribe to our e-mail updates so you'll know when new stories are posted."

About the story

The main concept of this story, that aborted foetuses have been given life without their mother's knowledge, is both terrifying and harrowing. In fact, I almost abandoned the idea after early drafts. Abortion is a complicated and sensitive topic, and it needs to be treated as such. I disliked Philip K. Dick's controversial story on the same topic, 'The Pre-persons', and was wary of producing something equally insensitive.

What made me persist with the piece was the ongoing debates about abortion laws in certain parts of the world. 'Choice' is an uncomfortable narrative, but it's also a pro-choice piece. Essentially, this story is an allegory for the injustice of a mother's choice being taken out of her hands. Although 'Choice' features complex characters, the only real villain in the piece is the company that took the choice away from the mothers.

The bleakness of this narrative is reflected in the setting: a half-abandoned Pyongyang in a reunified Korea. The unsettling atmosphere of this dystopian city is an eerie backdrop to such disturbing events. Much of my writing is inspired by the Korean peninsula, where I have lived for several years. The ever-complex relationship with the North, combined with the ongoing concerns about a rapidly ageing population, provide endless inspiration for speculative fiction.

The population issue comes into play here as an incentive for the abortion company to deceive families. The main characters' attitudes towards Korean reunification, meanwhile, provide telling insights into their personalities, which come to the fore at the story's climax.

A question for the author

Q: What's better: writing or having written?

A: Both are wonderful in their own ways. The writing process itself can be frustrating when things aren't flowing as you'd like, but the satisfaction after a successful writing session is hard to match.

About the author

Tomas Marcantonio is a fiction and travel writer from Brighton, England. His work has appeared in places such as STORGY, Twist in Time, and Lucent Dreaming. Tomas is currently based in Busan, South Korea, where he splits his time between writing, teaching, and getting lost in neon-lit backstreets.

@TJMarcantonio

Bedwyr by the Sea

C.B. Blakey

As the sun set over the sea, an old man built a sandcastle. His old green anorak sagged around him, patched and salt stained from years spent on the coastline. The sun glinted from the waves, so bright it was almost blinding. Eyes closed tight against the glare, his hands moved over the sand, pressing the crenellations into shape one at a time.

"Avalon," he whispered, feeling the sand firm beneath his fingers as he did so; the surface buzzing with static. "Avalon, Avalon, Avalon."

He worked slowly, trying to ignore the pain in his fingers and the nagging fear in the back of his mind. How many times had he done this in the last few years? It had only been once or twice a decade at first; now it seemed that barely a month passed that didn't find him kneeling on the sand, pressing the walls into shape beneath the waxing moon.

"How are you doing that, Mr. Bedwyr?" The old man flinched, letting out a gasp of dismay as the turret he was working on crumbled beneath his fingers.

"Oh, I'm sorry," said the voice. "Did I ruin it?"

"It's alright," Bedwyr rasped, praying that he spoke the truth. He scooped up more sand and hurried to repair the turret, his heart drumming deep in his chest as he fought to control the rising panic. His hands moved as swiftly as his swollen joints would allow, shaping and reshaping until all trace of the damage was gone.

Finally, he smoothed away the last imperfection and turned to peer out from beneath heavy lids. Standing a few steps away was a young girl, bundled against the chill autumn wind. Polka-dot Wellington boots sprouted from beneath a blue woollen overcoat that covered her from neck to knee. Only her head was visible, a ruddy-cheeked ball submerged in brown curls.

"Is it ok now?" Her voice was small and muffled by the coat. Bedwyr dragged the lake of his memory until a name emerged. Ivy, Ivy Winters. Looking past the girl, he recognised her parents further up the beach; a woman hurling a stick for a grey-muzzled springer spaniel while a man held a toddler's hands to steady him as he walked. Recalling his manners, he forced a smile.

"Yes, at least, I hope so," Bedwyr replied. "What were you asking?"

"I just wanted to know how you were doing that. I mean, you did have your eyes shut..."

"It's not so hard." In spite of his weariness, Bedwyr felt a surge of pride as he spread his hands out before him. "My hands know their work."

"What do you mean?" The girl frowned up at him. "I think you're cheating."

"Not at all," said Bedwyr, raising an eyebrow. "I have made this castle many times."

"I bet you haven't," said Ivy, gesturing towards the tide line with a sleeve that probably had a hand in it somewhere. "The sand's all flat here. Do you know why that is?" Her tone was deadly serious, so serious that Bedwyr found himself amused in spite of his irritation at being interrupted.

"I'm afraid I don't," replied Bedwyr, his voice shaking as he fought to suppress a chuckle.

"I do," she proclaimed. "It's 'cause the tide comes all the way up here. It'll wash your castle away easy. If you'd made it before, you'd know that." Her point made, she tried to cross her arms but had to settle for tucking one sleeve under the other.

"Is that so?" Bedwyr replied. "Maybe that's *why* I've made it so many times."

"Well that's just silly, why not make it by the path?"

"Because young lady, there are others who need it." The old man stared out over the water, squinting against the daylight. If he looked close enough, if the light struck the waves just so, he could see the crumbling walls.

"Fish don't need castles," said Ivy between giggles.

"Oh, I don't know about that," replied the old man, his face creasing into a smile. "You see them in pet shops all the time. That's by the by. I'm not making this for them." He ran a finger along the base of the wall. "This castle needs to be fit for a king," he whispered, more to himself than to anyone else, the tiredness creeping into his voice. "This one I make for Arthur."

"Arthur? You mean, like... King Arthur? The one with Merlin and the sword in the stone?"

"The very same." Bedwyr straightened up and eased himself back until he was able to sit with his legs stretched out. He looked out over the waves, breathing the sea air. "When I close my eyes, I can still see them. The boat was almost too small for them, if you can believe that. They had to crowd in like sardines."

"Is that why you're still here?" Ivy's question was innocent enough, but a shadow passed over Bedwyr's face.

"Someone has to keep the watch," he whispered. "Someone has to hold the route open." He rubbed his hands together, brushing damp sand from the calluses, then peered up at the sky. "There it is. You can't quite see it yet, but it's there. You know the moon's larger than normal tonight?"

"Mum says it's a special time," replied Ivy, a grin spreading over her face. "She told me this morning. She said it makes the wall between the worlds go thin, then dad made a joke about plastering and she got angry.”

“Nothing funny about plastering,” Bedwyr grunted. “She’s not wrong about the moon either. This is a good night to build the castle.”

“Where’s the drawbridge?” Ivy was regarding the castle with a cat-like intensity. Bedwyr blinked.

“Drawbridge?”

“Castles have drawbridges,” Ivy insisted. “If it doesn’t have a drawbridge then it’s not a real castle.”

“This castle doesn’t,” replied Bedwyr, slightly sharper than he’d intended. He took a breath to calm himself. He was a knight performing a sacred task; he was not about to sully that by having a blazing row with a child. “This castle doesn’t have a drawbridge, and I’m not about to add one. It has to be made the same way every time.”

“Why?” Ivy’s face radiated innocence, but something in her tone suggested that this question was a well-honed weapon indeed. “I mean,” she continued. “If you always make the same castle, how do you know you’re doing it right?”

"I just... you see..." Bedwyr paused, trying to find the words to convey the sense of rightness when he completed the castle, that this was something that you felt rather than knew. The words wouldn't come. Worse still, he could find no certainty that he was right; only the cruel edge of doubt that had shaded his thoughts over the past year. Bedwyr pushed it away; he was a knight, a warrior. He might be dressed in an anorak these days but some armour you never take off. He swallowed, steadying himself. "That's... just the way it is." The words felt hollow even as he said them.

"I'd want a drawbridge if I were the king."

"Well, we both know that isn't the case." Bedwyr regretted the words immediately, but Ivy didn't seem fazed by them.

"That's just boring," she mumbled.

"Boring has nothing to do with it," Bedwyr snapped, fighting to control his outrage even though he knew how ridiculous he must look. Worse, the words had struck a nerve. *Not boredom*, whispered a voice in his mind. *Fear.*

Bedwyr's hands balled into fists as the old memory surged into his mind. Once again, he remembered the sand caking under his nails as he traced new heraldry on the castle gate. Once again, he remembered the tide of panic that had engulfed him; the wave of fear that swept away the pleasure he took in his art. Try as he might, he couldn't recall the details of the decoration he had tried to add to the gate all those years ago; only the jagged hillocks of wet sand that remained after he had torn his ill-considered artwork apart. How close had he come to disaster that day? If he had let his changes stand, would the enchantment have been broken? Would his folly have condemned his comrades to death?

Maybe, whispered the voice again. *Maybe not. You don't know what would have happened. And if it had failed, if it had brought it all crashing down, at least that would have been an end to it.*

Bedwyr shook himself, relaxing his jaw. *This is foolishness*, he reminded himself. *Nothing happened. You fixed it in time. You made it right.* Besides, it had happened centuries ago, long before his skin wrinkled and his back ached. He looked down at his hands, scarred and swollen, remembering how they had itched to make something new, long before it hurt to move them. *Is this punishment*, he wondered? Had his desire to change the castle caused him to age so that he would be forced to carry out his duty with hands that barely obeyed him? He took a deep breath and pushed the thoughts away. If that was true, there was no changing it.

Abruptly, he realised that he had been silent for a long time and Ivy was staring at him. He unclenched his hands and gave what he hoped was a reassuring smile.

"This is my duty," he explained, his voice calm once more. "The final task laid upon me by my wounded king."

"Arthur got hurt?" The girl sounded more annoyed than shocked. "They didn't put that in the film."

"Well that's films for you," Bedwyr muttered, glad of the change of subject. "You don't always get the full story." The girl was quiet for a moment, staring down at her feet as she scraped her heel through the sand. When she replied, her voice was quiet.

"Will he get better?"

"Oh yes." Bedwyr offered her a smile. "He has to come back, you see. One day when Britain is in peril, Arthur will return to save us."

"But, won't that be dangerous? There's bombs and fighter jets now, he'll get blown up."

"Arthur will find a way, he must. It is the way of things."

"Does he have a dragon? A dragon could protect him from the fighter jets." Ivy was animated now, looking about wildly until her gaze settled on a stick about the length of her arm. She hurried over to it, pushed her hand free of her cuff and picked it up. Brandishing it like a wand, she leaned over and began to carve deep scratches into the sand in front of the castle.

Bedwyr was dumbstruck; he opened his mouth but no sound came out. Every instinct told him to reach over and seize the stick, that he had to put a stop to this immediately, but he couldn't move. *You want to see it*, whispered a traitorous thought. *You want to see what she makes.*

Paralysed by indecision, he watched as the dragon took shape before him. It lay before the gate, thick-limbed and long-necked with vast wings arching overhead; as long as the fortress was wide. Ivy straightened up and stared down at her handiwork, then leaned over and added a few small circles rising from the dragon's nose.

"What are…" Bedwyr's voice failed him. The panic he had anticipated was absent, leaving him feeling numb and hollow. He coughed and made to ask again. She answered before he could speak.

"Bubbles." The impish grin flashed from beneath the cloud of hair. "It won't be breathing fire underwater."

"I see." Bedwyr swallowed, sensing that he could no more stop this than he could the rising tide. "What colour dragon is he? Is he red or white?"

"She's purple." The grin spread wider.

"That's… unusual." He replied, his voice hoarse.

"Or course she is, she's a dragon."

"Ivy!" Her mother's voice cut through the conversation. "What have I told you about bothering people."

"Sorry, Mum." Ivy seemed to deflate, the stick drooping. Her mother, Bedwyr thought her name was Alice, hurried over and crouched in front of her daughter.

"We don't interrupt people when they're busy, do we?" Alice's voice was quiet, but firm.

"No, Mum," Ivy mumbled to her feet.

"That's right. Now what do we say?" Ivy was quiet for a moment before shuffling over to Bedwyr.

"Sorry, Mr. Bedwyr."

"That's quite alright, young lady." He raised his eyes to her mother and smiled. Alice seemed to relax a little, then let out an exasperated sigh when she saw her dog returning with what appeared to be a small tree clamped in its jaws.

"That's not your stick, is it, Cobb?" Cobb didn't acknowledge his mistress' voice, though the end of his tail wagged as he lay down to gnaw his latest acquisition. Alice tried waving another, smaller stick under the dog's nose. Cobb showed little interest, focusing all his attention on the branch; his eyes full of the fierce joy known only to dogs and drunkards.

Bedwyr watched them warily. It wouldn't take much; one fleeting moment of interest and the dog might decide to inspect the castle. He had encountered set-backs before; this wouldn't be the first time his handiwork had been demolished by an over-friendly hound. Only last year, a cocker spaniel had flattened half the walls and would have added a moat if the dog's owner hadn't intervened. He couldn't afford that today. The hour was late, too late to rebuild, and as he reached his hand towards the dragon, he could feel the crackle of static. For better, for worse, it was done. The dragon was part of the castle.

Slowly, Alice coaxed the dog free of his prize and led him back down the beach. Ivy followed her mother, the empty cuff of her coat sleeve flapping as she waved goodbye. Bedwyr smiled as he waved back, feeling the tension ease from his shoulders as they disappeared from view.

He turned back to the sand-castle, taking in the unadorned battlements and the sinuous wyrm coiled before the gate. Something was missing. The dragon did not seem of a piece with the fortress, and Bedwyr sensed that to leave things that way would spell disaster. A large part of him still wanted to reach out and obliterate it, to try and salvage what was left of his castle, but it was too late. Bedwyr stared down at the castle for a long moment, then his face broke into a grim smile. It was simple now. When all routes of escape are gone, the only path left is forward.

Grunting as his joints protested, he rose to his feet and moved along the shoreline where a thin ridge of shells met the encroaching tide. He walked slowly, eyes fixed on the ground, stooping again and again until his pockets bulged with shells and pebbles. His hunt complete, he turned and strode back to the sand-castle.

The tide was close now; there was barely time to complete his task. Heart pounding in his chest, he dropped to his knees beside the dragon. With shell and stone and wet sand, he anointed the walls and the wyrm that lay before them, binding them together till they seemed kin to one another. As he laid the final shell, a glittering shard that brought life to the dragon's eye, the sea reached the castle.

Bedwyr pushed himself away; his heels digging great divots in the wet sand. The water swept past the castle to pool around him, soaking his shoes and trousers. The sand around the dragon was pushed aside, the limbs, tail and wings rising and growing ever more life-like. The castle stood firm as the water receded, then the second wave came. Taller than the first and rose-tinted by the setting sun, it swamped the castle and its guardian. Sand sloughed away from the walls, billowing outwards in a great cloud to reveal glittering stone walls. The dragon writhed, tearing its head free of the sand. For a moment, Bedwyr found himself staring into a pair of eyes as old as the sea. Then the vision was gone. Fortress and dragon blurred together, then vanished as the water retreated, wiping out all trace of walls, turrets and dragon.

Bedwyr rolled onto his knees, then pushed himself to his feet, fingers sinking into the sand. He trudged up the beach till he was beyond the reach of the tide, then slumped on a mound of grass by the path to look out over the sea. As the sun sank below the horizon, a great band of gold appeared, reaching all the way to the beach.

Far below, Avalon slumbered, the great walls glittering in the light of the sun. Looking closer, Bedwyr could see that the walls had changed, now adorned with huge shell-like carvings and precious stones. A huge dragon lay curled before the gates, bubbles rising from its nostrils. Slowly, the golden band broke apart into individual patches of light and the vision of Avalon vanished. Bedwyr sighed, the weight of his isolation returning as the sea became opaque once more.

He closed his eyes, his head swimming, trying to grasp the enormity of what had transpired. He had built the same castle for centuries, duty and pride becoming tradition with the passage of time. It was as much a part of him as his hands or face, and yet he had allowed it to be changed on a child's whim. He kneaded his forehead, feeling a few stray grains of sand grate against his skin as his fingers probed his temples. It was then that he realised that the pain in his hands was gone.

He folded his hands together, bending and flexing his fingers, marvelling at how easily they moved. Rising to his feet, he took a few steps towards the waves, testing the movement in his knees and back. His joints moved easily. For the first time in over a century the simple act of walking was painless. As the tide retreated, it revealed a hollow in the sand where the castle had been, now filled with sea water. Cautiously, Bedwyr approached the hollow and stared down into a face he hadn't seen for a long time.

His cheeks were smooth, his eyes clear. Unbidden, Ivy's words floated through his mind. *If you always make the same castle, how do you know you're doing it right?* In a sudden flash of insight, he knew that it would be many years before he would feel the need to return and build the castle anew.

Picking up a flat pebble, he straightened up and watched the tide rolling in, savouring the feel of the stone as he rolled it between his fingers. He raised his arm and whipped it forward, sending the pebble skipping out over the surface of the water. His cheeks began to ache and he realised he was grinning. The new sense of freedom was so potent he felt almost dizzy, yet beneath it there was an odd sense of loss. Some part of him insisted that the castle he had built for so many years was gone forever.

No, the thought was a whisper, *not gone, just different*. The castle might have changed, but its walls were the same hard stone, its purpose just as important. Bedwyr turned his back on the sunset and walked up the beach to the path, his mind full of possibilities. He could go travelling, see the world as he had before. Better to go sooner rather than later, before people started asking questions. It was unlikely anyone would recognise him as old Mr. Bedwyr, but it wouldn't hurt to be careful. For a moment, he wondered how long it would be before he would have to return. Then he shook his head;

chiding himself. He would know when the time came.

Looking back over his shoulder, Bedwyr watched as the last light of the sun gilded the tops of the waves. Far overhead, a solitary gull cried out, the sound sharp against the hiss of water on sand. Bedwyr closed his eyes, listening. As the cry echoed amongst the clouds, he could almost believe it was a horn calling him home.

"See C.B. Blakey's story "Bedwyr by the Sea" online at Metaphorosis.
If you liked it, leave a comment. Authors love that!
Remember to subscribe to our e-mail updates so you'll know when new stories are posted."

About the story

"Bedwyr by the Sea" was partially inspired by a documentary (I forget which one) that speculated that the lost city of Avalon was a coastal city that has since been swallowed by the sea. The Arthurian legends have changed so much over the centuries that in many ways they are a fine example of stories that have evolved and thus remain relevant to modern audiences. I wanted to bring those two things together. Also, who can honestly say they don't appreciate a good sand-castle.

A question for the author

Q: Why do you write speculative rather than realistic fiction?

A: My love of speculative fiction is a disease that struck in childhood. When I was 7, my parents gave me a book of Greek and Norse myths and another of Arthurian tales. Ever since then I've devoured every fantasy novel I can get my hands on. When I started writing my own stories back in 2014, there was never a chance that I would choose a different genre. I love the freedom that speculative fiction provides, both as a writer and as a reader. Beyond the constraints of our own world, we can do anything.

About the author

A mythology nut and whisky enthusiast, C. B. Blakey lives in England with his wife, his daughter, and enough books to build a small fort. He writes fantasy and light horror short stories and will be starting a novel once he figures out how fit a few extra hours into the day.

Sonata I: Sona

L. Chan

Andante: Sona

Siege drums struck the town just before daybreak – whaleskin stretched over hollowed out tree trunks, varnished and polished until the drum bodies were darker than a moonless night. War Music was the province of the Empire military, and was not often employed by the Periphery patrols. Early morning mist clung to the ground, warping and distorting as the waves of force sped from the siege drums, propagating through the Sound and smashing into the town walls. Periphery grass was stiff, tough as wire, sharp enough to break the skin, same as the folk that lived on the Periphery. Unyielding, it shivered as if unsettled by a storm, though the still air held nothing more than music.

Sona didn't have to fight, but was up early to watch. Watching Sound in action reminded Sona of lazy evenings back at the academy, Sona watching others with more talent at instruments practicing. The Periphery was a great distance from the regional imperial academy where Sona had schooled, finishing as one of the top students in numbers. Accounting was hardly his calling, but his services were valuable to Grimheld and his band, and allowed Sona to tag along as the band made its way up the Periphery highway. The patrols were ostensibly aligned with the Empire, but far from the centre, the line between bandit and enforcer was faint, varying as capriciously as the weather.

Grimheld's band held a selection of siege drums, some trumpets, and a single bruised violin; barely a street corner ensemble back in the Capital. Out here, Grimheld fancied himself a Conductor, even if his motley assortment could manage nothing more than sections and movements from the Symphony of War. None of the great war machines, with their giant gears and pulleys operated by Sound. No air navy, with flyers held aloft by hot air and pushed upwind by huge propellers dancing to war music. Nevertheless, even a little war music put Grimheld and his men a cut above anyone else in this stretch of the Periphery. That and a little old-fashioned brawling was all they needed. Banditry in the Periphery worked similar to the collection of tolls or taxes. Some roughnecks held roads, preying on travellers. Others, like Grimheld, controlled swathes of territory, bleeding the inhabitants slowly.

The town's fortifications were ramshackle, guarding against the predations of normal bandits and thieves. Calling them walls would be generous; they were certainly not proofed against war music. As the drums played, vibrations travelled through the walls, sending ripples across stones larger than the head of a man. The wall heaved and bucked, masonry moving like waves on the high seas. A man's scream crept between the notes of the musicians. Someone had gotten too curious about the music, looking over the edge of the wall and taking the express route to the ground fifteen feet below. The movement reached its peak. Sona knew the staccato push and pull of the piece set up sympathetic vibrations in stone, the solid mortar liquefying and running like sand in an hourglass. All it needed was the push at the crescendo of the piece.

The music surged, and the walls came tumbling down.

Steel ringfenced the townsfolk, more edges around the weak and old than around the fighters; Grimheld knew how to control a crowd. The battle had been surprisingly bloodless – just two casualties from the town, falling off the wall. A few of the townsmen had blooded their blades, putting up a spirited defence and giving the raiders the odd scratch. Nothing that stitching and wine couldn't cure. Sona finished tabulating the ledger for the nameless town (surely the town had a name, the least of things had a name, even if it barely merited the ink it took mark it out on a map). The band had done well, turning out the limited riches of the town onto the dirt; imperial coin, other currency from up north; tarnished silver, verdigris-crusted brass — probably dowries or festival gifts.

Enough to feed the Empire, when they sent their people up here to get the pickings from Grimheld. The Capital turned a blind eye to the excesses of bands like Grimheld's, as long as tax kept flowing. Thieves, Sona had discovered, were particular about fairness, and he took care to split the spoils evenly. The townfolk watched in silence as their belongings were catalogued and divvied up. Empire game, Empire rules. If you played by the rules, the Empire always won but nobody got hurt. If you didn't, the Empire still won and everybody got hurt.

The accounts were presented in a hidebound book; the cut of the paper was amateurish, the pages oddly sized. But it held together and it worked, much like Grimheld's men. The Conductor himself was a small man, wiry and bristly like the most resilient of terriers. Those who tried found him quick for his fifty years, accurate with both rapier and dagger and, despite his formal title, devoid of all but the most minuscule musical talent.

"So this is your last town with us," said Grimheld, licking a finger and running it down the column of tiny numbers. Sona nodded. This was for show; Grimheld was both illiterate and innumerate. The previous quartermaster had skimmed the spoils, his own personal tax. Grimheld had eventually found out and the band had gained a barely competent, one-handed cook. Sona became the new quartermaster, appointed despite being unable to speak since infanthood. So the young man dressed in the scarves and high collars of the Capital rose from part time instrument tuner to full time accountant.

Sona winced as Grimheld scored the rough paper with a facsimile of the characters that comprised his name, his signature never twice the same. "I have something for you, come." At the older man's gesture, Sona followed, leaving the ledger on the makeshift table wrangled from a hearth or kitchen, adjusting with wind numbed fingers the dirty scarf around his neck.

The Conductor brought Sona past the townsfolk to a set of six prisoners, wrists manacled. The six did not wear the braids of the Periphery, but instead covered their hair with silk headscarves. Though faded with distance from home, the six women still wore the sun of the Far Isles on their brown skin, and were dressed in rough travelling linen after Periphery fashion. Sona bit his lip. Slaves. Slavery was banned in the Empire Sound; apologists pointed to the Empire as offering a fairer rule for all men, but the truth was much more prosaic. Slave revolts were as messy as they were common, and paying servants was cheaper than paying soldiers. Far away from the capital, where swords far outnumbered slaves, principles were harder to come by.

"You've been honest with me, and that's a rare thing on the edge of the world. So you get to choose. Choose and keep, but just one, mind you. I'm not that generous," said Grimheld.

Five had fresh parchment skin, teenagers but with soldier's eyes hooded and perched atop dark pouches. Number six was past her middle years, with a strange focus to her gaze. Like the other five, she'd seen war and pain. But she'd come out of that shared experience hard. Hard and angry. Sona was going further north, up into harsh steppeland. A translator, if any of the six were so inclined, would be useful. He just had to find those that understood Fingerspeech.

Fingerspeech was common in the Capital. As many as two in five were fluent, and all who were at the sharp end of the Empire Sound spoke it; deafness was rife amongst those who dealt death through war music, common amongst the workmen that wove music into the industry that pulsed through the arterial roads, airways, and seaways. But Sona was climbing up the fringe of the Empire, far from the active fronts. Soldiers were rare, Imperial Common took on the throaty slur of the north, and Fingerspeech was barely to be found. Grimheld was off to the side, joking with the guards, something raucous and bawdy. Sona kept his hands low. It would not do him any favours for the mercenaries to see how Sona chose his payment.

Of the six, only the oldest blinked twice. Sona had found his translator.

A quartermaster had privileges, privacy being one. Sona's tent smelled of sweat, and of the animals that carried it up the

Periphery roads, but it was his and his alone. In a crowded encampment, this was a luxury. In the middle of the room sat his travelling chest, a bespoke thing of inlaid mahogany and teak, bound within the guts of a brass multipede. The musical multipede was the centrepiece of the room. It served as workspace when fully expanded, but was now locked in the dismount position, its eight legs folded, double jointed like a beetle's, brass pistons and copper gears oiled and dormant.

We have some time to discuss the terms of our arrangement before they will expect noise, Sona said, continuing to converse in Fingerspeech.

What arrangement? Am I not a slave? she asked back. *We do not even have each other's names.*

The Empire has no slaves, said Sona. *You can call me Sona.*

Sona for Sound? Empire name, Empire lies. But not Empire skin, she said.

Half Empire. My mother was of the Six Named, he said over his shoulder, using one handed Fingerspeech, the tactical sort favoured by soldiers. The blood of the Six Named was strong, not easily watered down. His skin remembered the harsh sun of the Northern Steppes, his hair black and wavy. He wore Six Named blood on his face: his nose wide, forehead broad and eyes dark. But Sona did not hold himself like the horse-riders of the north, his posture stiffer and crisper than a dress uniform; a far cry from the soft slouches of his mother's people, bodies bent to absorb the constant footfalls of the shaggy beasts that carried them.

The woman shuffled in front of him, the chains of her restraints dragging like a tail. Sona pulled at his filthy scarf, showing the scars at his neck. *There's no need to get in front of me. I can hear just fine; these scars are all that is left of my voice. We have business to discuss,* he said.

"State your business, Sona of the Empire. Don't you even need my name?" the woman said, switching to Imperial Common, the tongue spoken through much of the Empire and its vassal states.

There's no need, I can't call your name. We are to go north, to the Nation of the Six Named. I have business there at the Festival of Names. You will speak for me, and you will be compensated for your time, he said, laying a stack of Imperial crowns on the edge of the multipede's gaping maw.

"And if I refuse?" she asked, voice low, hoarse. Sona went back to packing, kneeling in front of the multipede.

I cash out my last payment from Grimheld's band, you join your companions. They will sell them and you, and Grimheld has no hold on his men to keep them from sampling the merchandise, he said, not even looking up.

Sona managed to get one hand in front of his windpipe as the woman slipped her manacled wrists in front of his face. "What is to stop me from killing you in your sleep, or right now, Sona of the Empire? My time is worth more than a handful of crowns, and there is not enough money in the world to pay me to do Empire business."

There was no sound in the room, save the woman's heavy breathing as she pressed her knee into Sona's back, cutting off his air with her chained wrists. At least the guards wouldn't be suspicious at the sounds from his tent. Sona tipped his head back, exposing his neck, tempting the woman to double the pressure. There was a click as the manacle popped open, the iron bracelet barely clearing Sona's chin as the woman lost her footing and stumbled backwards.

If you will not take coin, then a blood debt instead, Sona said, holding up a slim key, with his free hand.

"I'm listening," she said. Sona tossed her the key, she snatched it out of the air with her free hand without looking.

First amongst the animals in bravery is the field rat, a creature that will feign death if caught. So strong are their wills that they will not flinch even if an animal takes a bite from their living flesh, all the while waiting for the right time to bolt. I need at least one of your companions to be that brave. All will die otherwise, he said to the unchained woman.

"The least of them is that brave. But why should I trust you?" she asked.

Because you have no choice.

"I am Shailani. We have an agreement."

Journey by multipede was perhaps one of the worst ways to travel. The multipede took her toll on the backsides and spines of her riders. Instead of steaming breath, the multipede was powered by Sound. A marvel of horology and music, the rider simply pedalled, driving a mechanism which played an extract from the Symphony of Industry, just a few bars, but enough to provide the force to run the gear shaft which pumped the legs of the multipede. Gearmusic, the horologists called it. Musicians and Composers in the Empire treated it with disdain, but mechanical music was the backbone of Empire industry and the Empire war machine. Sona had never liked gearmusic much; he resented the soulless tedium of the repeated notes.

Solitude was a companion Sona had missed. He had been content to travel alone between Empire cities. At least there, field justices appointed by the Emperor kept brigands in check. He had taken the long road from the clock city Pendulos, where he'd lain low after fleeing the Western Academy, as his mother had told him to. There, as new skin grew over burnt flesh, he plotted, immersing himself in his mother's research, before setting out for the Periphery. Mingling with the tradespeople and pilgrims, the Empire road had been boringly safe. The road along the Periphery to the Steppes up north was equally long but infinitely more interesting. Sona had been forced to choose between being victim of the uncontrolled banditry of the trade highways or of the controlled banditry of Grimheld and his contemporaries. Bartering his services to the strong had been Sona's only way of paying for safe passage.

The slow travels around the western reach of the Empire and up to the northwest had grated on Sona; all the more so when he was carrying his prize. In Pendulos, he had taken up his mother's research, melding the clockwork sciences of Pendulos with the theory of Sound. But tinkering was not enough for his plan. The Six Named land was the next step; the conversion of knowledge into power. And with power he could strike back. Back at the Lord Antius Deathsinger, the man who had made Sona what he was. Sona was uninterested in the machinations and intrigues of the Houses of the Capital, about revolution and power, but he was owed blood, and he would collect.

Dust clouds bloomed under the multipede's brass feet, flat and splayed like those of a camel. Shailani drew her headscarf across her nose and mouth, one hand still holding onto the multipede's saddle for support. The chains had been off since they'd put two days' ride between them and the town. Sona hadn't bothered to learn its name. In his accounts he'd just numbered towns off on a map, reducing brutality to a series of columns and sums.

We should eat, he said, bringing the multipede to a halt, tune dying to silence. Shailani wobbled as she took her first steps. Multipedes did that to you, pounding away your sense of balance, step by shaking step. While she swayed, one hand on the brass fittings of the multipede, Sona laid out their shared provisions, noting that both water and food had dipped below the halfway mark. Hard bread, hard cheese, hard jerky. The water which he poured into two stained copper cups was itself stale, and had taken on the sharp bite of metal from its receptacle. Shailani looked at the sun nearly overhead, turned to the right so that her shadow was behind her, knelt, and bowed twice, leaving a smear of grey dust on her forehead.

You are a captive in a strange land, and still you give thanks for your food? he asked.

"I am not hurt, and my portion is the same as yours. There is much to be thankful for," she said.

And the two bows? he asked, before sawing at the bread with a short dagger. The blade was barely a finger's length, and had seen combat. If Sona looked closely enough, there would still be blood crusted at the choil, but he hoped Shailani wouldn't notice.

"Thanks to the spirits. Once for me, and once for you." When Sona's eyebrows raised, she carried on, "I'm a captive, not ill-mannered."

We don't have gods in the Empire, Sona said.

"It must be lonely, then," replied Shailani.

Gods are for the weak; the land is here, the Empire is powerful because of the strength of people, not because of any spirits.

"Ah yes, Empire strength. Greatest in the continent. Can your Empire sing the sun to rise in the morning? Did it sing creation itself into being? The Empire has no soul, and that is why it will end."

Without an answer, Sona pushed Shailani's portion of bread and cheese towards her. He said, *If we had returned to camp, I would have offered you mango jam from your Far Isles.*

"My sister-children have never tasted sweet mangoes; the best of our lands is taken to garnish the Empire's tables. I think the bread is enough for me," said Shailani.

Empire wheat, milk, and pig, Sona said, gesturing at the food in turn. *Nothing from Far Isles here. Anyway, we don't steal from the Isles. We trade with your Sultanate.* The Sultanate was the de facto power over the raucous, archipelagic Far Isles.

Shailani winced as she bit. The crunch of the stale bread was audible, doubtless rattling her teeth in her head. She drizzled water on her bread, softening the chunk. A soldier's trick.

So how does a Far Isles woman become proficient in Fingerspeech? asked Sona. *Tactical Fingerspeech too.*

"The isles are only far when one considers the Empire at the centre of everything. If you honour me, you would at least call my homeland by its name," Shailani said, her cheeks colouring, crumbs spraying.

Sona chose his words, fingers moving over each other deliberately, each gesture perfectly crisp. *Your land has no other name in the Empire,* he said. *You are of the Sultanate, are you not?* Nominally so, since nearly every island in the region had its own tribe, with very particular ideas about whom it owed allegiance to.

"Those the Empire cannot conquer, it befriends. But Empire only knows Empire, and its friends are very much like it. Before the Empire came to Seribu, the Sultan only ruled half the territory. He bartered aromatic woods, gemstones, and rare beasts for imperial instruments. Now the Sultan controls it all. Including my people. Have you heard of the Sixty-Seventh regiment?"

That word you used? Sona asked.

"Seribu? It means 'the thousand' in my tongue. The true name of the Far Isles. You don't even care enough to have a name for it in Fingerspeech."

And then she was silent.

So Shailani was from the Sixty-Seventh – the Irregulars. Sona looked her over again, taking in the details he'd missed earlier. The way Shailani moved, light on her feet and balanced. She'd kept the woman's robe of the Periphery, but sashed it tighter around knee and elbow, making sure the voluminous cloth wouldn't trip her.

Deserted? Sona asked.

"Discharged after twenty years, with full colours. I made sergeant. You know what happens to deserters."

So, a decorated veteran. The Empire military was one of the few that had women serving. All the way since the reign of the Emperor Regent Ophelia some thirty years prior. With most of the heavy lifting done by Sound, physical strength was only valued for close quarters brawlers and cavalry. Still, prejudice ran deep and few women made sergeant, fewer lieutenant, and none above in a generation. Getting as far as sergeant meant that Shailani had other skills besides Fingerspeech.

And you got captured by a mongrel outfit like Grimheld's, said Sona.

"Trading us lessened the toll on the townsfolk. I had five to protect and no good options. You would have done the same," Shailani said, and when she tore the last of her bread in half, her knuckles were white under skin.

You don't know me. You are far from home. I assume you have business up north, pressed Sona.

Shailani made a show of chewing the tough bread, jawline sharp under her headscarf. "You've yet to tell me *your* business, Empire boy."

When it is time, said Sona.

"Taking without giving in return. You've not got Empire skin, but you've got Empire bones. Let me guess. You're not tall, but that's the Steppes in you; good bones means good nutrition. So you've seen money. You can stop me anytime I'm incorrect."

Sona began packing, keeping his hands busy to avoid answering.

"You have tools and ride a multipede, so you've got some craft in you. Maybe apprenticed to a horologist. Falling in with a band of mercenaries isn't straightforward, so I assume you understand war. Not enough scars to be battle tested, so I'd guess academy training."

Sona hated reminders of the time at the academy. If he closed his eyes, he could still smell the smoke.

The Western Academy was in flames; the burning front was a living thing, leaping from tapestry to rafter and back again, cutting off escape. His mother, the Lady Kristyk, was visiting. She'd found her way to his dormitory, past raiders, past fire. Not unscathed. One arm was blackened and peeling, the other holding one of her blades, the point tracing a scribble in the air.

"They'll not tell one body from another in the ashes. Leave your necklace and rings." Her voice a rasp from the hot smoke. Sona did as he was told. Shouts down the corridor, getting closer.

You go ahead, mother, I can manage the corpse, Sona said urgently, smoke obscuring his Fingerspeech. His roommate was a year younger, but Sona had always been small for his age.

"Hide on the Steppes, never come back to the Empire. There must be no doubt of your death. When you get there, tell Fong that the debt is repaid. Go."

We have to go, said Sona now, fingers crisp and sharp, the memory of acrid smoke making his nose itch and his eyes water.

The village could barely be called that, the stones that made up its walls rough and irregular, the inhabitants likewise. Harsh wind, hot off the Steppes, blew ochre grit into tiny vortices and curlicues, blasted it into wall and face alike. Hot food was a bonus, but the bread was not much better than the chunks they'd been eating on the road. The stew was a lumpish grey, root vegetables boiled down into a powdered mush, meat either clumps of gelatinous, wobbling fat or thin strips of gristle.

The innkeeper introduced himself as Druck, showing a mouthful of teeth at odd angles and with a time limit on their tenancy in his mouth. Sona and Shailani retired to their room. He gestured to Shailani to take the bed; he'd grown too used to hard ground on the road and even the straw filled mattress would leave him with a backache. Besides, he had work to do.

They struck in the early hours of the morning, at least an hour past midnight, but the Periphery lacked good clocks and time here was malleable.

Two of them, by the moonlight coming in through the window Sona had left open despite the desert chill. Gesturing to Shailani's sleeping form, the pair did not notice Sona emerging from beside the doorway, not until he'd brought the pommel of his short knife down forcefully on one shadowed head.

The man dropped with a grunt, and his partner spun, longsword at the ready. Few of Grimheld's band had fighting experience outside of bar room brawls and the gutting of unarmed innocents. This lent itself to flamboyant gestures, like bringing field weapons for indoor fighting, and, when confronted with the slumped body of a comrade, demonstrations of strength, like a two-handed overhand strike with a longsword.

Sona darted in quick, mindful of the body at his feet, one stiffened forearm a roof over his head, ready to shunt his attacker's strike down past his side. Unnecessary, since the tip of the sword bit deep into the thatched rafters and stopped. The tip of Sona's dagger found its way, through force of habit, to the armpit of his opponent, the spot traditionally uncovered by plate armour. Not that anybody could afford armour out here anyway. The attacker's eyes rolled up in his head. Brum. A pity. Brum had always been polite and good for a game of dice. The ledger was in Sona's favour, if he recalled. Perhaps the man was pettier than he'd let on.

Sona was still wondering if the spray from removing the dagger would dirty his travelling clothes when someone tackled him from behind. His head struck the edge of the bed on his way down, vision going white at the edges before he hit the floor hard. Breathing was impossible. Something on his back, maybe a knee. A rough hand flipped him around, and Sona felt the pressure of a dull blade at his throat, his assailant pinning him down by the simple expedient of straddling him, pinning arms by his side, squeezing air from his lungs; the cook, and former quartermaster, was a large man. Apparently, the band was out to settle all accounts with Sona before he left Empire territory.

"Hello Sona," said the cook. "Been waiting a long time for this. Not so chatty even without your tongue up Grimheld's arse, are you? Oh, I forgot."

Fingerspeech required at least one arm to be mobile; Sona was at a disadvantage and merely made a rude gesture with each hand.

"You've cost us five slaves. We knows it was you that done it. Nearly got them back, we did. Managed to get one in the leg with an arrow drum, but she was smart, that one. Lit a campfire all on her own and let her sisters sneak twice the head start on us." The cook drew the tip of the rusty knife down Sona's neck, dimpling skin. If the cook had been any more disciplined about upkeeping his blades, Sona's skin would have parted easily. "Maybe I'll be quartermaster again after yer gone. Cookin's not my style and dressing meat's hell for a man with but one hand. I should get some practice in." The tip of the knife drifted down, pressing through Sona's clothes; a shallow stab, just enough to keep Sona's attention.

A meaty slap cut through the silence, Shailani's fist appeared at the side of the cook's neck. The man shuddered, flesh jiggling. "Up now, big boy and lose that little pig sticker you got in my employer," she said. "What you have in your neck is something we call a lintah, a leech blade. More of a tube than a blade, really; a lot like a spigot in a beer barrel. You're going to want to get your hand up here." She clucked at the cook when his hand twitched, pulling his head back to make her point. "Slowly. Good. When I take my hand off, you're going to want to put your thumb over the hole. Good. Hold it there and we'll leave the beer inside the barrel, eh?"

Sona teased the blade free from his chest. Blood leaked but did not spurt. Good; he hadn't travelled this far to be laid low by a man like this. He nodded to Shailani. She turned her attention back to her captive, circling around him.

"The leech can bleed you fast or slow," she said. The cook took a half-hearted swipe at her with his other arm, the one to which he'd fitted an evil looking hook sprouting from a leather harness. His motion elicited a spurt of fresh blood from the knife in his neck. "Don't move, don't talk. I just need you to blink, once for yes, twice for no. Can you do that for me?"

The cook blinked. Sona had seen the man dish out his share of cruelties on the band's victims. Many of them looked a lot like the cook did now, sweat beaded on a furrowed brow, eyes white all around, breath shallow and rapid.

"The four others, are they being pursued?"

Blink. Blink. A single tear leaked from an eye, followed the furrow of an old scar, got lost in the half globe landscape of his sweaty chin.

"The one that was wounded, did she die unsullied?"

Blink. A rapid calculus of the costs of deception. Blink.

"Good boy. One more question, if you please. Did you partake?"

Blinkblink.

"Thank you," said Shailani, and kicked the cook's hand.

I thought they searched you, said Sona. They were downstairs packing up. The innkeeper was in his own bed, eyes wide and dry, divining the secrets of the ceiling, throat ragged and open to the night air. Cook and friends had been too clumsy to sneak by the innkeeper and too cheap to pay him off. Shailani pulled her headscarf back, revealing greying hair knotted into a simple bun. Even in the half-light, Sona could see the fan of thin tubes, leech knives as hair ornaments.

Not soldier's weapons, Sona said.

"Anything that kills is a soldier's weapon. We should stock up," she said.

That would be stealing, said Sona, before gathering his belongings. His

Fingerspeech was barely discernible past the shaking of his hands.

"It's funny you say that, just after killing a man."

You've killed before, he said.

Shailani looked away, breaking line of sight and silencing Sona. "Enemies. Friends. It's just meat. No memories, no family, just meat. Easier that way, helps me sleep."

She turned back. "I need more than guesswork. You let me have the bed because they'd go for it first. I know your type. We had Empire officers in the Sixty-Seventh, but only the commissions who couldn't pay their way out of the front. Most were snivelling little snots. When we sent some of the bodies home, not all of them had wounds in the front. So let me ask you, Sona of the Empire, what is your business with the Six Named?"

Sona paused, then exhaled a week's worth of tension in a long sigh, shoulders slumping. He waved Shailani over to the multipede, brass legs folded and compartment gaping. Grunting, he lifted several heavy boxes out of the way, eliciting metallic clangs of complaint. Those boxes were individually locked, by coded mechanisms rather than by keys.

Their secrets were not for Shailani, not yet. His mother's secret masterwork, perfected by Sona and the horologists the Lady Kristyk had paid to hide Sona after her death.

Another hidden panel hid Sona's treasures. Two stacks of paper. The first, a stack of letters unsent, written in script so neat it might as well have been printed. The pile grew more slowly the further Sona got from the Capital, the less he thought of his sister. Letters never to be sent, not as long as those behind the Western Academy fire thought he was dead. There was a spike of guilt when he thought of Canta. Although just a half-sister, they were close enough in years that they had been tutored together. His sister had inherited his father's height, her laugh booming and free, her punches faster and stronger than their teacher's. He wondered, as he always did, what terror she'd be up to back in the Capital, where they used to sprint across the moored airships at the Skydock. Sona pushed the letters, and his memories, aside.

Instead Sona drew forth the second set of papers, sheet music in the hand of the Lady Kristyk, her other masterwork. The rustling of the papers and the guttering oil lamps made the notes dance on their ordered lines. Sona paused. He was taking a risk here, disclosing this to the old soldier woman. Shailani would be the first person he'd shown the music to. Yet trust had to be won somehow. His fate would be in her hands when they got to the Six Named land. Better to start now.

There is a time of gathering up north for the Six Named. All manner of people, he said, one-handed, holding the music out for Shailani to see. The woman scanned the music with the quick glances of one skilled in reading music. The Festival of Names was an annual affair, something he'd only heard of from his mother. Each sept would send their elders to consult the Book of Names, to choose names for the newborn and to strike off the names of the dead.

"Looking for a wife?" Shailani asked, showing a little too much interest in the music. Sona jerked the sheets back. The festival was a time for unions as well. There was no better time to leave one sept for another, save that they did not bear children with any who shared one of their Six Names. Everything else was fluid –

rearing of children, hunting, farming, border patrols, craftsmanship.

It was not marriage Sona sought, but music. *I need this played for me. Played by people I can trust. People not of the Empire,* he said.

"That's a lot of music, a full movement. Which Symphony?"

Not one of the four, he said. The Symphonies of War, Industry, Order, and Flow were the backbone of the Empire Sound. Each held the movements of music that ran battle, agriculture, the artifices of the city, and physical combat. Each symphony the province of one of the Maestri; each Maestro lording over a House with the power of a small country.

Sound was all around the world, a force of nature; even animals had use of it. But nobody on the continent used it like the Empire, and the tools of the Empire were the Composers—the few souls in with the talent to pluck notes from Sound, and weave those notes into music, and the music into each of the Symphonies. The Symphonies were the property of the Empire, and those that could command it even more so. Sona was a player of average quality; perhaps suited for industry or the civil service. His strength lay in his tinkering with gearmusic and with the music of the Symphonies. The Lady Kristyk had guided him with his tutors, careful for Sona only to demonstrate average facility in musical theory.

All empires gestated the seeds of their own undoing, although most were more subtle about it than the Empire Sound. It was an act of conceit that the Empire took its name from Sound; a power available to all, a power that it abused and feared. And because the Empire feared, it controlled, forbidding all music but that of the Symphonies. The Empire assigned each of the four Maestri a Symphony, each great house controlling the Composing and use of all Sound within its Symphony.

"Dangerous business," said Shailani. "Illicit Composing is sedition, high treason against the Emperor himself." Sona said nothing, but slipped a tiny assassin's dagger from his sleeve and palmed it.

You've got an eye for music, said Sona. *Not just some foot soldier.*

"Battle choir, section leader. I know my Music, Empire boy."

Now you know what I need done up north, are you still with me? asked Sona, waiting for Shailani to hesitate, to give him a single reason to mistrust her. None came.

"My sisters are still free. Our agreement holds. Hide your music. You can see to provisions. One of your old friends is still alive in the next room." She stepped up to Sona, close enough for her breath to tickle his lashes. When he retreated, she seized his hand and relieved him of his dagger. "You get this one for free. Best get used to killing, boy. Looks like your business will see more before it's done."

🗡 🗡

Stay tuned for part II of Sonata in next month's issue!

"See L. Chan's story "Sonata I: Sona" online at Metaphorosis.
If you liked it, leave a comment. Authors love that!
Remember to subscribe to our e-mail updates so you'll know when new stories are posted."

About the story

"Sonata" is one of the longest things that I've written (and completed). I don't often work in the fantasy sandbox, I much prefer near future science fiction and contemporary fantasy. For "Sonata", what preceded the story was the world building — a magic system that fell roughly as another aspect of the physical world, and where the control of that magic ran along political and societal faultlines rather than through resource or genealogical lines. Things flowed on from there — an extant Empire with a colonialist reach, a good old fashion revenge quest and some non-traditional characters. It didn't get really steampunky until about halfway in, when I realised that the frame of having a sound based magic system would overcome a lot of the engineering limitations of steampunk without pushing the rest of the technology of the world into the industrial revolution or thereabouts. It was also important to me to retain a tight cast of characters this time round, although the roster is definitely going up if I ever return to these folks.

A question for the author

Q: What inspires you?

A: Many things! I'm the filter feeder in the inspiration food chain. Sometimes, it's bouncing ideas off tweets with friends. Sometimes I start with a title but no story. Sometimes I start with a line or a scene with no idea how the rest of the story goes. Recently, I've tried to address some weird imbalances in tropes that irked me, like the Selkie myth.

About the author

L. Chan hails from Singapore. He spends most of his time wrangling two dogs. His work has appeared in places like *Translunar Travellers Lounge, Podcastle,* and *the Dark*. He tweets occasionally @lchanwrites.

lchanwrites.wordpress.com

Copyright

Metaphorosis Publishing

Metaphorosis offers beautifully written science fiction and fantasy. Our imprints include:

Metaphorosis Magazine
plant based press
Metaphorosis Books
Driftwyrd
Vestige

Help keep Metaphorosis running at
Patreon.com/metaphorosis

See more about some of our books on the following pages.

Metaphorosis Magazine

Metaphorosis

Metaphorosis is an online speculative fiction magazine dedicated to quality writing. We publish an original story every week, along with author bios, interviews, and notes on story origins. Come and see us online at magazine.Metaphorosis.com

Keep Metaphorosis running! Support us at
Patreon.com/metaphorosis

You can also find us at:
Twitter: @MetaphorosisMag, @MetaphorosisRev, @Metaphorosis
Facebook:
www.facebook.com/metaphorosis

We publish monthly print and e-book issues, as well as yearly Best of and Complete anthologies.

Metaphorosis:
Best of 2018

The best science fiction and fantasy stories from *Metaphorosis* magazine's third year.

Metaphorosis
2018

All the stories from *Metaphorosis* magazine's third year. Fifty-two great SFF stories.

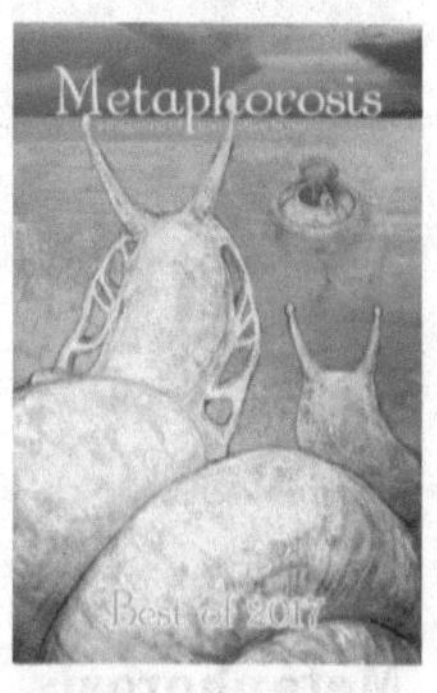

Metaphorosis:
Best of 2017

The best science fiction and fantasy stories from *Metaphorosis* magazine's *second* year.

Metaphorosis
2017

All the stories from *Metaphorosis* magazine's second year. Fifty-three great SFF stories.

Metaphorosis:
Best of 2016

The best science fiction and fantasy stories from *Metaphorosis* magazine's first year.

Metaphorosis
2016

Almost all the stories from *Metaphorosis* magazine's first year.

Plant Based Press

Vegan-friendly science fiction and fantasy, including an annual anthology of the year's best SFF stories.

Best Vegan SFF of 2018

The best vegan science fiction and fantasy stories of 2018!

Best Vegan SFF of 2017

The best vegan science fiction and fantasy stories of 2017!

Best Vegan SFF of 2016

The best vegan science fiction and fantasy stories of 2016!

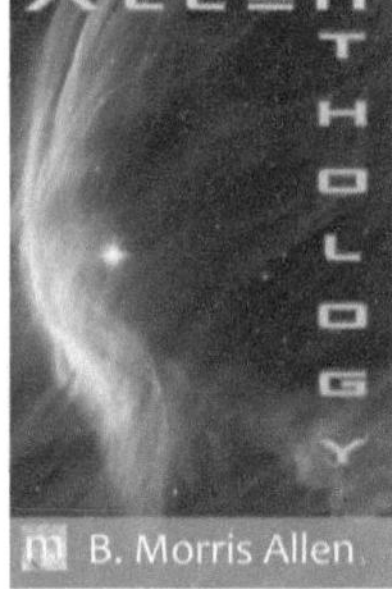

Susurrus

A darkly romantic story of magic, love, and suffering.

Allenthology: Volume I

A quarter century of SFF, including the full contents of three separate collections.

Metaphorosis Books

Science fiction and fantasy books for writers – full of great stories, but with an additional focus on the craft of speculative fiction writing.

Score

an SFF symphony

What if stories were written like music? *Score* is an anthology of varied stories arranged to follow an emotional score from the heights of joy to the depths of despair – but always with a little hope shining through.

Reading 5X5

Five stories, five times

Twenty-five SFF authors, five base stories, five versions of each – see how different writers take on the same material, with stories in contemporary and high fantasy, soft and hard SF, and a mysterious 'other' category.

Reading 5X5

Writers' Edition

All the stories from the regular, readers' edition, plus two extra stories, the story seed, and authors' notes on writing. Over 100 pages of additional material specifically aimed at writers.